THE SAXON
GAMES

SPECIAL FORCES
V
SOCIAL MEDIA

For Derek-

With very good wishes

THE SAXON GAMES

SPECIAL FORCES
V
SOCIAL MEDIA

NORMAN HARTLEY

For Vanessa

Editor and muse extraordinaire

ALSO BY NORMAN HARTLEY

The Viking Process
Shadowplay
Quicksilver

The Saxon Network

WHO ARE THE SAXON NETWORK?

The Saxon Network is a group of friends who rallied round former SIS intelligence officer John Saxon when he was wrongly disgraced and accused of murder.

The key members are:

'Tim' SAS Squadron Sergeant Major Tim Overton. Fieldcraft expert and former sniper. Served in Northern Ireland, Iraq and Afghanistan. Rescued by John Saxon from one of Saddam Hussein's torture centres in Iraq.

'Kate'. Kate Allison. American round-the-world yachtswoman. Tough and daring. Doesn't give a damn for the rules. Now John Saxon's girlfriend.

'Chunk' The initials of SAS Major the Right Honourable Charles Hubert Ulysses Nigel Kingsland-Manderby, DSO, MC.' Dresses like a Christie's art auctioneer. 'Wealthy, sporty, Oxford-educated, and as adept at violence as any tearaway in inner London.' Currently at the Ministry of Defence.

'Lottery' SAS Sergeant David Salmon. An outstandingly brave fighting soldier who 'whenever he gets into some crap situation mutters that if he ever wins the lottery he will give all this up!'

'Birdy' Lieutenant-Commander Jonathan Sarum RN. Ninth generation navy. Helicopter pilot and daredevil. Got his nickname after clipping a tree top while flying low to impress a girlfriend. Told the CO it was a bird strike – but admitted the bird was in its nest at the time. Currently attached to the SAS.

'Rachel' Detective Chief Inspector Rachel Hunter, Metropolitan Police. Tim's girlfriend. Former Coalition police adviser in Iraq, now serving in inner London. Street-wise and razor sharp, noted for 'interrogation room eyes'.

'Bob' Bob Cronin Ex-CIA technical officer, chemical and germ warfare expert, served undercover in Iraq as weapons inspector. International bridge player.

PROLOGUE

When I was half-way over the Channel, I did a victory roll in the Tiger Moth. I was alone and there was no-one watching. I did it for sheer joy. It was a long time since I had felt so free. I was no longer a disgraced SIS intelligence officer, forced to hide under an assumed name in the BBC. The deal worked out by MI6 to keep me out of an Italian jail for alleged murder was history. The wheel of fortune had spun and I was back on top again.

It had happened by accident. My arch enemy Ray Vossler, the Washington financial crook and ex-CIA consultant responsible for all my troubles, had walked into the BBC World Service newsroom because his current mistress had a fancy to see it. That had set in motion a train of events that had completely turned the situation around but I certainly hadn't done it alone.

I had been saved by a group of friends, most of them serving in Special Forces, who had become known as the Saxon Network. They had rallied round me, risking their careers, and together we had wrecked a plot by Vossler to launch a bio-terrorist attack on London and have it blamed on Iran. Now, Vossler and his associates were in jail awaiting trial and I had just had a wonderful holiday in the United States with my new girlfriend, Kate. With her agreement, I was now on my way to France to attend the wedding of an old friend in the company of my ex-girlfriend, Marie-Hélène, which promised to be very entertaining.

For the hell of it, I did another roll. Life was good. Everything was going right. How little I knew what was in store!

1

I lay on a double bed in the Auberge des Fleurs as Marie-Hélène undressed, deliberately too close for me to avoid watching. She had suggested sex and I'd said no because of Kate, but she was making a point of reminding me what I was turning down.

It was a strange situation. We must have made love a hundred times in this same bedroom but our affair had ended, quite amicably, four months before. Now we were together again because the owner of the Auberge, Jacques Mercier, was getting married and was throwing a huge party for all his friends and regular clients.

It would have been rude to refuse the invitation and we had agreed to meet platonically but Marie-Hélène had connived with Jacques for us to have our beautiful, spacious old room, overlooking the Auberge's miniature lake. Everything about it was familiar. We had our habitual sides of the bed with our own drawers and parts of the wardrobe and we even knew where we would each charge our cell phones. Yet, it was all different now because I had fallen in love with Kate. Marie-Hélène knew that and she had decided to tease me.

'It's obvious you're not French,' she said, with a grin as she took off her bra. 'Anyway, don't you have a saying in journalism, 'what happens on the road stays on the road.'

'I'm not a journalist anymore,' I said, trying to keep the tone light. 'I've resigned from the BBC.'

'Aren't spies even worse?' She laughed. 'Especially a famous spy who has come out of the shadows to become a national hero.'

'I'm a hero on the internet. You know how much that means.'

'Nonsense, you're a national hero. You and your so-called network saved London from a germ warfare attack.'

I smiled. 'That doesn't allow me to be disloyal.'

'I won't tell her! This can just be a passing fancy, a recreational weekend. Would she really care?'

I knew Marie-Hélène would not be happy until she knew more about Kate - she was a barrister and it was her style to question forensically in private as well as in court.

'Did you know that in French a thong is 'un string'? she said as she adjusted the few centimetres of black silk around her thighs.

I smiled. 'Yes, I do know.'

'Of course, you do. And I remember now. You don't like thongs much do you? I'll have to see what else I can find to wear.'

She waited for me to make a move but when I stayed where I was she shrugged.

'Well, if you don't want me, I'll have a quick shower then we can go for a walk and you can tell me all about her.'

When she was in the bathroom, I got off the bed and went over to the window. Below, the town band was rehearsing for Jacque's wedding lunch the next day. The marquee was already in place on the hotel lawn and catering staff were unloading tables and chairs and placing them in groups round the edge of the lake. I heard Marie-Hélène turn on the shower and I wondered what her next move would be.

In normal circumstances I knew I would have given in to her tempting but the truth was I was now too happy to take the risk. I would never have admitted it to Marie but secretly I was quite enjoying my hero status, however temporary it might be. I was also relieved to be out of the BBC. I had really enjoyed my time at the World Service but the quiet, orderly life had begun to get to me. I had no idea what choices lay ahead, but I intended that there should be some excitement. Life was good and I wasn't planning to spoil it by being lured back by Marie-Hélène.

She came out of the bathroom wearing a few hundred grams of multi-coloured silk which almost made a complete dress and she looked absolutely gorgeous. Yet there was definitely something different about her. She was still as stylish as ever, but she seemed to have toned down her usual elegance. Usually, she always looked ready to be photographed for *Vogue*, even on holiday. Now, her look was more casual, and she seemed genuinely more relaxed.

'I thought you might have joined me in the shower like you used to,' she said, playfully flicking the hem of her skirt in my direction, 'I was quite looking forward to making love to my first spy.'

She gave a mock sigh. 'So it's just a walk and time to tell me all about your new life!'

The bedroom had its own staircase leading from the balcony down to the garden. We walked down, exchanged a few greetings with hotel staff busy on the lawn, then strolled into the wood at the side of the hotel, until we were almost out of earshot of the band. Following our old routine, I had flown the Tiger Moth that morning from Headcorn in Kent to Boulogne and Marie-Hélène had taken an early TGV from Paris. As I had left the Tiger parked on a grass strip at the back of the hotel, we walked over for a quick check. Usually, it didn't attract much attention as it was a familiar sight, but many of the wedding guests hadn't seen it there before so Jacques had had some makeshift barriers erected to keep back the curious.

'So are you officially a spy now?' Marie-Hélène began.

'No, not at all. I'm not BBC any more, obviously, but I'm not MI6 either. The problem is that legally I've been rehabilitated, but MI6 has no idea what to do with me. My ex-controller, Virginia Walsh, would like to see me buried in a deep hole and forgotten about but there are talks underway to decide whether or not I can have any kind of return to the organisation. It's a fine legal point. I've been told I could argue that my dismissal was entirely contrived and I am actually still an employee.'

'Do you want that?'

'I honestly don't know. There are some things about the old life that are tempting but I can't see how it could work.'

'And what about the lovely Kate?'

'Limbo again but a different kind. We've had a holiday in Gloucester, Massachusetts, and I have met her family.'

'Where is she now?'

'She's in Weymouth covering the sailing Olympics for an American magazine syndicate.

'So that means when you leave here, you can have a nice romantic seaside holiday.'

I laughed. 'In my dreams! Kate is going about covering the Olympics the way she goes about everything else, full on. I'll probably have to drag her by the hair to get her to join the party occasionally.'

'What party?'

'The network is gathering in Weymouth for the Olympics. We haven't seen much of each other lately. Tim has been running an SAS training exercise in the Welsh mountains. Rachel has been tied up with a big case in London. Lottery has been back on base in Hereford and as Chunk's father is seriously ill, he's been tied up with family matters.

'What about your hero helicopter pilot friend?'

'Birdy? He's in great form. His flying exploits have gone viral and he's being offered the loan of helicopters right and left. Of course, he's a sailing fanatic too. He's already in Portland. His girlfriend's in Singapore now but she wants to try and get back to join us.'

'You'll still have the nights with Kate and plenty of time for sex.'

I laughed. 'It took quite a bit of wheeling and dealing for us even to share a bed! The syndicate she's working for, Ocean Reports, wanted to charter a huge cruiser as their base but Kate said she wasn't going to live on board a floating cocktail lounge. We've ended up with two rather sleek but pretty cramped yachts moored side by side. Tim and Rachel and the gang will be in the other one. I at least managed to convince Kate that I wouldn't be too much of a distraction if I shared what is laughingly called her cabin. The rest of the boat is a floating workspace.'

Marie-Hélène laughed. 'I'm sure you'll manage, knowing you. Is she good in bed?'

I laughed too. 'You know me better than to ask that.'

'No I don't, I'm French. I can ask if I like.'

'But I don't have to answer,' I said, still smiling.'

Marie-Hélène detected the slight hesitation my voice, which suggested there was more to tell.

'But?'

'But Kate is keeping her distance emotionally. While we were in the States it was terrific. It was a true holiday with sex to match. Time out from the real world. Now, she's a bit like MI6; she doesn't know what to do with me.'

'And what do you want to do with her?'

'I'd like to be with her.'

'You mean get married?'

I smiled. 'I wouldn't dare breathe the idea, she'd be half easy across the nearest ocean before I could get down on one knee!'

'But do you want to?' Marie persisted.

'Not yet, no. Maybe not ever. It's just that it's different now that I'm myself.'

I could feel the impact this would have on Marie-Hélène as I spoke. Throughout all the time she and I had been together, I had been living a lie, under a false identity, and she had never really known anything about me. Inevitably it had made our affair superficial. I wanted something different now, but I didn't want to hurt Marie-Hélène by admitting it. But she was quick, as always.

'You mean you want to try a proper relationship now that you don't have to masquerade as BBC editor John Cartwright.'

'Something like that. But if I know Kate, I'm going to come a very poor second to the sailing for the next little while.

'I liked John Cartwright,' Marie-Hélène said thoughtfully. 'You played the role pretty well.'

'Only pretty well?'

'Most of the time. No that's not fair, nearly all of the time. Just occasionally you stepped out of character.'

I looked at her curiously.

'Like when?'

'Do you remember that time in the nightclub in Paris when that mean-looking guy tried to chat me up and turned nasty when I said no? When you faced him, I've never seen anyone sober up and back off so quickly. And I could see why. It was the way you stood absolutely calmly, knowing there could be a fight but not in the least bothered by the prospect as though it was a minor nuisance but the outcome was a foregone conclusion.'

'I did my best to be kind and gentle,' I said, 'but I obviously let the mask slip occasionally. Kate said once that I sometimes walked around the newsroom as though I was looking for something to kill and eat.'

We walked on until we had reached a clearing. It was another familiar spot. We had made love here not so long ago but there was no point in looking for somewhere without any personal memories. The grounds of the Auberge and the surrounding woods had been our world for too many memorable weekends.

Marie-Hélène was walking slightly ahead of me, not attempting to hold hands. I watched her, trying to work out exactly what was different about her. She had let her dark hair grow much longer since I had last seen her and she had left it free and loose. Yet she was different in other ways too. She had always made such a production out of grooming and styling but now she seemed totally at ease in her own skin.

'You've changed,' I said.

'Yes, I have.'

'Any special reason.'

'A very special one. I've left my father's firm.'

'What! You mean left altogether?'

'It's the biggest decision I've taken in my entire professional life.'

She smiled. 'A lot has happened in the past two months. I didn't tell you because we were no longer together and anyway you had concerns of your own.'

'It sounds serious.'

'Oh yes, it's very serious. I've broken with my family. Not just with the firm. I couldn't stand being under my father's thumb any more, professionally or emotionally.

'Why now? What happened?'

'My father wanted to make me a partner.'

'That doesn't sound very threatening.'

'But it was. He wanted an ally he could control. He had no plans for me to have any increased independence or status. He wanted another vote so he could dominate the management board. He made that perfectly clear. He has always dominated me and my mother and I mean totally.'

'Did you have to make a full break?'

'I decided I'd had enough. I resigned - from the firm and from the family. I'm now no longer Marie-Hélène Demonteuil, I'm plain Marie Cassia.'

'The name you always use here at the Auberge.'

'That was just discretion at first, then habit. In fact it's my mother's maiden name. Marie is one of mother's family names too. My father insisted on adding the Hélène, a name which comes from his side of the family. I dropped it to make the break complete, so that's what you must call me from now on.

'What will you do?'

'I'm taking a career break, but only a short one. Then I'm going into a practice with an old friend, a woman I knew in law school. We're teaming up with two English women who are setting up their own practice in London. We're planning to attract some pan–European business.'

I knew she had spent two years in London during her legal training. She hadn't been called to the English bar but she was very proud of the fact that her English was flawless.

'Sounds as though it's going to be a very different world,' I said.

'It certainly is. I'll miss the fees but not much else.'

'Will you take any of your clients with you?'

'A few, but only the ones my father won't miss. For the past two years he's been giving me the cases that involved social networking or the media. He hates all that stuff. We're going to make it one of the new firm's specialities.'

She laughed. 'One of the nice things about being around you is that you aren't interested in Facebook and Twitter.'

'I could hardly have a social network presence when I didn't exist.'

'But what about now?'

'Now's even worse. The whole network has been swamped by new, so-called friends. Kate's become so irritated even she has abandoned Facebook and Twitter for the time being. The whole world seems to want to be part of her life.'

'Yes, I noticed she's gone quiet.'

'You've been looking?'

'Of course. Anyway, shouldn't you be calling her?'

'Cell phones are another problem,' I said. 'Our numbers got out and we were deluged with pointless or intrusive calls. Jay, our technical wizard, has set us up a private network on different phones. But don't worry, mine's switched off. If it rings, that means someone is using the over-ride and they won't do that unless it's something really urgent.'

'Not even Kate?'

'Especially not Kate. She's totally wrapped up in the Olympics. I managed to see her a bit at the opening ceremony but now we're into the Games proper, I wouldn't dare disturb her. I'll call her later. For now, let's just enjoy being here.'

She took my hand and squeezed it.

'I am enjoying it,' she said, 'it's been rather a tense time and I was looking forward to a relaxing weekend but if you're sure you need to be

English and stay faithful to your new girlfriend.... even though she won't commit emotionally.'

I smiled. 'I'm sorry. Maybe I am too British.'

'How about a good luck kiss anyway. That surely doesn't count as infidelity even in England.'

She drew me close and as we kissed, she contrived very skilfully to make contact with my body from forehead to ankle.

'Does good luck normally involve quite so much tongue?' I said when we finally drew apart.

'Of course. That was to wish me luck but it was also the first of your tests.'

'What tests?'

'Think of yourself as a mediaeval knight. You've given your favour to the lovely Kate, now you have to face challenges to prove your worthiness.'

'And these tests are what exactly?' I asked, playing the game.

'You have to conquer the demon lust,' she said. 'I'm role-playing the demon for the next two days.'

When we reached the edge of the grounds of the Auberge, Marie sat down on a grass, and motioned to me to sit opposite to her.

'If you won't talk to me as a lover, talk to me as a lawyer, she said, 'tell me exactly where things stand with you and your enemies.'

'Superficially, everything is going fine,' I said. 'Ray Vossler, Simpson Carr and Ali Omar have all been charged with conspiracy to commit an act of terrorism and have all been refused bail. Vossler has appealed twice already but given his wealth and standing he is a very obvious flight risk and hasn't succeeded.

'And under the surface?'

'Several things make me a bit uneasy,' I said. 'The case is going to be very complicated. Ray Vossler masterminded a germ warfare attack on London. He used three Iranians as front men and his plan was to get Teheran blamed for the attack and damage relations with Iran irrevocably.

'We foiled the attack but we agreed to keep quiet about some of the details in order not to create panic and show how near London came to a major disaster. I'm a bit afraid they'll be able to use that to muddy the waters in some way.'

'And what else?'

'If I know Ray Vossler he'll certainly try and find some way to blame everyone around him and claim that he had only a subsidiary role, when he was in fact the mastermind.'

'If the judge has any sense, he won't wear that one easily,' Marie said. As she spoke she adjusted her knees so that I could see straight up her skirt. The glimpse of black silk was discreet and fleeting but quite deliberate.

I smiled. 'Was that another test?'

'I'm not sure I understand you,' she said with mock coyness.

I don't know how many tests I would have passed but I never got chance to find out. My demon was obviously going to be very persistent but before we could resume the conversation, my cell-phone rang.

It was Birdy. The conversation was short and tense.

'Kate's been hurt,' he said, 'is there any way you can get back?'

'What happened?

'A man tried to grab her on the marina. She managed to struggle free but then she fell into the harbour and he escaped.'

'How bad is it?'

'There's nothing broken. A lot of bruising on the arm and shoulder from hitting the boat. She's OK, but she could do with a bit of TLC.'

'Did she say that?'

'Of course not. But I believe she does need protection. I have a real feeling it was not a random attack. I'm pretty sure they're going to try again.'

2

When I flew into Weymouth the next morning, the last thing Kate wanted was tender loving care. She was furious, frustrated and prepared to resist anyone who tried to wrap her in cotton wool. It didn't take me long to find out why. I landed at the farm building near Chickerell where I'd found a hangar for the Tiger Moth for the duration of the Games and took a taxi to the marina to take over from Birdy, who didn't want to leave Kate. When I arrived on board the *Jurassic Star*, the boat that was Kate's base for the Games, the doctor had just left and she was spitting feathers.

'Stupid patronising old git,' she spluttered.

'He only wanted you to have an x-ray,' Birdy said soothingly.

'I don't need an x-ray. I'm not going to spend all day waiting around some hospital. There's nothing broken or dislocated. He agreed didn't he?'

'Doctors need to be sure.'

'Well I'm sure.'

Finally, Kate turned to me. 'You're back early. What happened to the wedding?'

'It's going on today. Marie is representing both of us. I thought I might be able to help here.'

'You should have stayed,' Kate said. 'I'm fine and we're going to carry on as normal. Just let me get on with my work. Do you understand?'

I smiled. 'Don't I even get a welcome hug?'

'No you bloody don't. I hurt too much.'

'I thought…', I began, but Kate cut me off.

'I'm not having an x-ray and that's final.'

'Kate's probably right,' Birdy said. 'She's black and blue around one shoulder, along one arm and in part of her midriff where she scraped the side of a boat before hitting the water. There are several pretty deep cuts as well but as long as she's careful, she should be fine.'

'I am fine. Look, is there any way we can put off this bloody policeman who's coming. There's a briefing in less than an hour and I'm nowhere near ready.'

'We can't stop him, he's on his way,' Birdy said, 'but we'll try to keep the interview short.'

'There shouldn't need to be another interview. I told everything I know to that idiot child of a constable who came yesterday.'

'I think the idiot child is the problem,' Birdy said.

He turned to me. 'The guy who's coming is Inspector Andy Frampton, and he sounded pretty sharp, more's the pity. The constable who came yesterday was just a kid and he assumed it was a random mugging.'

'And it wasn't?'

'Oh for Christ's sake, don't start this again,' Kate said angrily. 'Birdy is convinced it has something to do with Vossler. If that idea gets around we'll have a social networking circus and the hacks already here will be all over me.'

'I know that,' Birdy said calmly, 'we mustn't even hint to Frampton that it might be anything but a casual assault, but trying to duck the interview is not going to help.'

Birdy glanced at his watch.

'He'll be here shortly. Shouldn't you put your sling back on.'

'I don't need it,' Kate snapped.

'Yes, you do,' Birdy said gently. 'I'm not trying to coddle you. I'm trying to get you fit to carry one covering the Games.'

'I'll put it on later, after he's gone. We're supposed to be playing the whole thing down aren't we?'

'Fair enough,' Birdy said, 'but do rest the arm whenever you can.'

Before I'd had time to get any more details of the attack, Inspector Frampton arrived and I knew straightaway he wasn't going to give us an easy ride. He was a lean, wiry man in his mid-thirties. When he introduced himself, he showed us his warrant card and began very formally, referring to Birdy as Lieutenant Commander Sarum and me as Mr Saxon.

We sparred politely and learned he had been born and raised in Portland, and that he was a keen sailor and knew a lot about Kate's expeditions.

That was all fine, but by the time we were on first name terms we had gathered that he had followed all of our recent adventures in London right up to Ray Vossler's arrest and knew a great deal about both me and

Birdy as well as Kate. He was here, he said, because the constable who had taken the details after the incident was not local, and had been very recently transferred in.

'Constable Waterford assumed it was some kind of sex attack or attempted theft,' Frampton said, 'but that doesn't seem to make a great deal of sense. It's an odd time of day and an odd place for a random sex attack or a mugging - very public, no cover and a fair number of muscular blokes around the marina to intervene.'

'Which they didn't do,' Kate objected.

'No, but help came pretty quickly once you were in the water. We have to assume that if someone had tried to rape you on the quay, there would have been rescuers. Also, you were in sailing gear. Hardly likely to be carrying a load of cash dressed like that. No hand-bag to snatch, no jewellery, probably a mobile phone but there are much more likely places to nick phones.'

No-one responded so Frampton continued with his train of thought.

'But if we assume it wasn't a sex attack or a mugging and it wasn't random, then we have to look at reasons why you should be a target, Kate.'

Again no one responded until Kate said, 'if you're assuming it has something to do with the events in London, then why should they target me, not John, or Birdy, or one of the others?'

Frampton shook his head. 'I've no idea,' he said, 'but we have to look at the possibility.'

'If word gets out that you're taking that line,' I interrupted, 'there'll be a joyous media circus. For the national press it will overshadow the games coverage.'

'And it will make my life hell on wheels,' Kate added, 'I'm going to have enough trouble covering the Games with this,' she tapped her shoulder, 'but if the rest of the press start chasing me about it would just be impossible.'

'I understand all of that,' Frampton said quietly, 'and there won't be any leaks. I'll make damn sure of that. The last thing I want is a media scrum. I'm really pleased Weymouth got the Games and I won't do anything to disrupt them. But I must do my job. If you were the target, the attacker could try again and I can't turn a blind eye to that.'

I could see that Kate was quietly coming to the boil. She was already imagining some kind of police protection or restrictions on her movements and she wasn't going to have any of it.

I intervened quickly. 'You don't have to worry about Kate's safety,' I said, 'I'm here now. Birdy is staying too and by tomorrow there'll be at least two more members of our team down here.'

Frampton smiled. 'The famous Saxon Network is re-assembling, is it?'

'Not re-assembling, only partying. Everyone's managed to get a few days leave and we'll be watching the sailing and having a few drinks. It's just a celebration get-together, but you can be very sure that we'll look after Kate if she does turn out to be in any danger.'

I saw Kate bridle at the idea of being protected and went on quickly, 'but I'm sure there'll be no need.'

Frampton seemed quite satisfied with that and I thought the interview was over, but he had other ideas. He had already arranged with the marina manager to look at the CCTV footage of the incident and wanted us to come with him 'just in case we recognised the attacker.' It was going to be a tricky moment. If we did recognise anyone, the last person we would tell was Inspector Frampton. The inspector might be able to keep his own ideas on the investigation quiet but if we identified a possible suspect he would have to make some kind of a written report and the chances of a leak would multiply.

'I haven't time to come,' Kate said. 'If this has anything to do with Vossler and his crew, John will recognise them better than I would.'

'The Vossler crew, as Kate calls them, are all in jail pending trial,' I said, 'so it's not likely to be them.'

'Nevertheless,' Frampton said, getting to his feet, 'let's go and take a look, shall we?'

'We won't be long,' Birdy said to Kate. 'As soon as we get back, we'll drive you to the briefing straightaway.'

The marina offices were very close to our mooring and the manager was ready for us. He was friendly and efficient; he knew Frampton and had the CCTV tapes ready.

The pictures showed the incident exactly as Birdy had described it. Kate had been walking along the quay with her friend Sally who had stopped to speak to somebody on a nearby boat. Kate had walked on alone and a man had come out from the side of the marina building, grappled with her and tried to drag her away. Kate had fought furiously and almost broken free but the man had kept hold of one arm. In the wrestling that followed Kate had managed to disengage her arm but by the time she succeeded, she was at the edge of the quay and had slipped between two boats into the water. On the way down she hit her shoulder against the bow of one of the boats and scraped herself on the mooring line of the other one.

When we had finished watching, I was the first to shake my head.

'No, sorry, no one I know.'

'Nor me,' Birdy added.

I think we were convincing even though we both instantly recognised the man who had grabbed Kate but I couldn't tell whether Frampton believed us. We shook hands and Frampton gave us a card with his direct number and we assured him we would contact him if there were any developments.

That was Kit Sanders, wasn't it?' Birdy said when Frampton had gone.

'No doubt about it.'

Sanders was a British contractor who had worked with Ali Omar for Ray Vossler in Iraq and Jordan.

'And Mike Waugh.'

'You saw him too?'

'I wouldn't have, but I followed your eyes. As soon as you recognised Sanders, you started looking nearby.'

'Just habit. Do you think Frampton noticed?'

Birdy shrugged. 'I don't think it matters. He's no fool. He could see that Sanders was trying to drag Kate towards the exit at the side of the offices. That would take them right out into the marina car park. Even though he couldn't know Waugh, he would assume someone was in a car waiting. No-one in his right mind would try to control Kate alone.'

'I made it a Ford Focus, dark grey.' I said.

'Yes, pity we couldn't see the plate.'

'Lucky for us Omar is still in jail,' I said. 'He wouldn't have botched it. Sanders is good, but he's past his best. He did a twelve-year hitch with the British army. He's been well-trained but he's not the fittest specimen around.'

'Waugh's not much better,' Birdy said. 'The word is Vossler likes to use them both because has some kind of hold over them which keeps them nice and loyal.'

'So what do we do?'

'We take damn good care of Kate, whatever she says. They're going to try again aren't they?'

'You can bet on it,' I said. 'Sanders isn't going to go back to Vossler and say, sorry Guv, she fell in the harbour.'

'What's behind it? Why Kate?'

'Not sure,' I said. 'She's the first here, most vulnerable, easiest to pick off.'

'Best way of putting pressure on you most like. Whatever they want, they know you wouldn't break easily. Kate could be their best bet.'

The session took no more than thirty minutes but when we got back to the *Jurassic Star* there was no-one there except a photographer called Jason.

Kate's gone to the Sailing Academy for a briefing,' he said casually.

'Why didn't you go with her?' Birdy snapped.

'Sorry, I offered to drive her because of the shoulder but she refused. She got quite cross. Insisted on driving herself.'

'Come on,' Birdy said, 'we need to be with her.'

We reached the Sailing Academy within ten minutes but we hadn't realised how strict the Olympic Games security procedures were. Half a mile from the entrance was a perimeter gate manned by two civilian security guards and two soldiers checking credentials. Birdy showed his Navy ID card but was told that wasn't enough. They were apologetic but had strict orders to allow in only press. We backed away from the gate for a quick consultation and decided Kate would probably be safe inside and there was no point in creating a scene. There was a layby a few yards from the gate and we pulled in to wait. Kate's car was not hard to spot. It was a silver Honda with Ocean Reports stencilled on the side. It was nearly an hour before she appeared but she drove slowly towards the gate and was easy to flag down. As she came out, I could see it was painful for her to drive but that didn't make her pleased to see us.

'What's the matter?' she said. 'What's happening?'

'Kate, you know why we're here.'

'Yes, I do, and I'm not having it. I'm not going to treated like a first grader who has to be met from school.'

'I'm not going to argue,' I said, getting in beside her. 'If we have to fight it out, we can do it back in the boat.'

Birdy took his car and I wanted to drive Kate but I knew that wouldn't work so I sat quietly beside her and watched her struggle tight-lipped with the steering wheel. I could see this was a row I would have to end up winning, however much bad feeling it caused, but the fight was postponed by a phone call that Birdy received a few minutes after we were back on board.

'It's Bob Cronin,' he said. 'He's on his way and he wants us to get everyone to Weymouth as quickly as possible for a briefing.'

'I have to be in London tomorrow,' I said. 'It's my official meeting with MI6. I can't miss that.'

'Well get back as quickly as you can. Cronin says it's too complicated to explain by phone but there's a serious chance things are about to go tits-up.'

3

By eleven the following morning, I was sitting in the Chelsea home of Chunk, or more correctly, Major the Right Honourable Charles Hubert Ulysses Nigel Kingsland-Manderby, DSO, MC, examining his latest acquisition, a set of Indian throwing knives and a gold-encased target studded with jewels.

'Why don't you try them out?' Chunk said, 'they're almost perfectly balanced.'

'I wouldn't dare, that target looks far too valuable.'

'Probably as well,' Chunk said. 'It was designed by a Maharajah. If he thought one of his warriors was getting above himself, he was invited to demonstrate his skills. If he hit a jewel, he was executed.'

The knives had just been added to Chunk's astonishing collection of ancient weaponry which over the years had turned his elegant town house into what could have been one of the most interesting museums in London had he ever opened it to the public. Each time I visited, I was introduced to some new and usually elegant tool of violence. My favourite was another Indian weapon, a Bagh Naka, an assembly of curved blades designed like a Tiger's claw to slash through skin and muscle. Chunk used it as a soap dish.

Chunk's nickname was based on his initials but there was an extra twist. He had a most un-Chunk-like lithe, almost willowy figure and dressed more like an art auctioneer than a highly respected SAS officer who was known to be fearsome in combat.

'So tell me about this attack on Kate,' Chunk said as he handed me a coffee.

I told him everything in precise detail, including our identification of Sanders and Waugh.

'Is Kate still mad at you?' Chunk said.

'She is sort of generically mad at everybody. But we did make a kind of peace this morning.'

This time, I didn't go into detail because our reconciliation had been both unexpected and very enjoyable. I had spent a chaste night trying not to accidentally roll into her. We were sharing what was known as the State Cabin on board the *Jurassic Star* but its double berth was only double if you slept really close and Kate was in no shape to be curled around. Eventually, I had found a sleeping bag and stretched out on the floor beside her.

During the evening we'd reached an uneasy truce. She had worked most of the time and we had gone out for a drink and supper at The George on the quayside. We hadn't argued but we hadn't made up either. I wasn't sure how the morning was going to begin and it was a pleasant surprise to be woken by a gentle hug and a kiss on the back of the neck.

She had said simply, 'thanks for leaving me the bed. It made a real difference,' adding, 'I'm sorry I was such a bitch yesterday. I know you were only doing what you had to. I always react like that. I can't help it. I've had to fight so many battles with my father and my brothers.'

I'd said I understood, but adding with a smile, 'All this celibacy is going to be the end of me.'

She had smiled and kissed me again, sending me off to London with a hug and a promise, 'Don't worry. It won't last for ever.'

'And this call from Bob?' Chunk asked, bringing me back to the present.

'Haven't a clue,' I said, 'but doesn't sound good.'

'OK,' Chunk said, 'let's put all that aside for the time being and concentrate on today.'

He smiled and gave me an odd look.

'What?'

Chunk went on smiling. 'Nothing. I was just trying to picture you as an intelligence bureaucrat.'

'That's not necessarily what they'll offer me,' I said, trying not to sound defensive, 'if they offer me anything at all.'

Today was to be my first face-to-face contact with MI6, an interview to set the seal on my so-called rehabilitation. It wasn't going to be the last word on my future but it would be a critical meeting.

'How do things stand at the moment?' Chunk asked. 'Has Sir Alastair worked his magic?'

In the weeks since the arrest of Vossler, I had dealt with my former employers only through my solicitor, Sir Alastair Stewart.

'Alastair is satisfied that the documents handed over by the service have removed any possibility of my being extradited to Italy,' I said. 'With what we've got, no court could ever put me on trial for murdering that Italian lieutenant. They are four credible witnesses on record saying it was an accident.'

'And the rest?'

'No idea,' I said. 'My future with MI6 is still totally up in the air.'

'So how do you like to see yourself? Chunk asked, 'undercover again in Iraq, Syria, Jordan? My dear friend, you are one of the best known faces on the internet. It will take more than a touch of make-up and a white robe to hide you.'

I had been quietly dreading this conversation, but Chunk was the one person I could trust to look calmly at all the options, speaking as a friend but also analysing forensically and ruthlessly with no concession to my feelings.

'Is the Chief still in Washington?' Chunk asked.

'Yes. I've no idea what he thinks about me,' I said, 'I doubt I'll find that out today.'

The Chief of SIS, Sir Jeremy Peacock, had been appointed after I had been kicked out. His own speciality was Asia, and especially China and our paths had never crossed during his early career.

'I'm seeing his deputy, Mark Worricker. And of course, you can bet Virginia will be there.'

Virginia Walsh was my personal nemesis in MI6. She was roughly fourth in the hierarchy of the Service and was aiming to go higher but her position had grown shakier as she was the one who had orchestrated my phoney 'exit in disgrace', which had now blown up in her face.

'Worricker is a decent enough chap,' Chunk said, 'but he won't take any decisions without Peacock's say-so, so let's take Virginia first. You have to decide whether you want to try to make peace with her, or go on treating her as the enemy.'

'I'm open to a truce,' I said, 'but it'll be up to her. She doesn't do regret and she'll only support me if she feels it will help her own cause.'

'That's true,' Chunk said, 'I gather she's busy rebuilding her own position and she fights a mean fight.'

'Is she winning?'

'Struggling a bit, I gather. Also, things aren't going too well at home. Her accountant husband seems to have gone off on a tour of the world's tax havens. The word is he wants to stay out of the way until he sees how she comes through this.'

'A real hero.'

'Oh yes. He doesn't want to catch any downdraft if she comes unstuck.'

'Will she come unstuck?'

'Too early to tell, but there's no point in worrying whether she'll help until you decide what you want her help with.'

I smiled. Trust Chunk to go for the jugular - in his gentlemanly way of course - knowing I wasn't likely to get what I really wanted, the post I was really qualified for, Director of Middle East Operations. He also knew that I was unlikely to enjoy going back at a lower level to wait for a senior job. It was not a good position to be in for today's meeting.

Chunk voiced my doubts without needing to be prompted.

'Let's be realistic,' he said, 'you'd make an outstanding Director of Middle East Operations but they're not going to give you that. At least not yet. The question is, could you stand the bureaucratic life?'

'I can't see them sending me back into the field.'

'No, nor can I, but anyway do you really want to?'

'Probably not'

'Which doesn't leave you a great deal of choice.' Chunk grinned. 'Still, I wouldn't start applying for jobs at Tesco yet. The service might just come up with something really interesting. I'm told that Peacock is pretty imaginative. Get him on your side and you might be surprised.'

Chunk stood up. 'Let's go outside. It's cooler there.'

We walked out into the courtyard and into a blaze of colour. Another curious side to Chunk's character was that he was an expert in growing clematis and there must have been thirty varieties in the small walled garden-cum-court-yard. Chunk claimed that he was too lazy to learn how to grow more than one flower and had chosen clematis, but typically, he had made himself an expert and created a notable collection.

His other gift was to have ensured that he was left alone by his neighbours. Chelsea was notorious for ridiculous feuds between arrogant, wealthy residents but Chunk had managed to convey in his usual mild-mannered and charming way that he was not a man to go to war with.

'How are you fixed financially?' he asked, as we settled into two luxurious garden recliners.

"OK,' I said. 'BBC salary has stopped, of course. I wasn't asked to work out my notice. HR is still trying to work out how to handle the fact they employed someone who didn't actually exist! I've calculated that I can afford to give myself up to three months to look around – if I have to.'

This had been true when I made the calculations but there had been developments in the previous couple of weeks that had made me slightly nervous. My friend Clive had called me to say that the Tiger club subscription and insurance charges were going up and that anyway, our plane was due a service, which would not be cheap. I'd also learned that I was going to have to pay for an expensive repair to my flat and that my children's school fees in Canada were also likely to go up.

I knew Chunk could hear the reservation in my voice but he didn't comment directly.

'Had any job offers?' he asked.

'Half a dozen corporations operating in the Middle East have offered me consultancies.'

'No-one you fancy?'

'Possibly, if I get desperate.'

'What about Academe? Can you see yourself as Professor of Middle Eastern Studies somewhere, in the States possibly? You're supremely qualified. Or a UN Special Adviser, that sort of thing? Or a Think Tank? Plenty would have you, and you could combine it with a nice line in punditry, or a newspaper column. You're not going to starve.'

I laughed. 'No, but I might just keel over from boredom.'

'There is that, but what about Kate?'

'Oh God,' I said, 'don't make the situation more complicated than it is already.'

'You are in love with her?'

'Yes, I suppose I am, but I don't see any way we can have a future together.'

Chunk gave me one of his wry smiles.

'You could always be an honorary woman on one of her all female expeditions. Or you could become a home-maker and welcome her back from the sea from time to time.'

I laughed. 'That's about the size of it. It's a very modern problem. Two lovers, two careers, need I say more?'

'Are you ambitious?'

'I don't want to climb any particular ladder but I do want to do something worthwhile, something which has a point.'

'In a word then,' Chunk said, 'you are stuffed. 'I think it's time for a glass of champagne. But don't worry,' he added, 'we'll make sure you don't get stranded. There are plenty of interesting options if you know where to look.'

It was a great note to end the conversation on but the mood was broken by a vibrating beep on the special cell-phone that our technical adviser, Jay, had provided. The call was from my solicitor, Sir Alastair Stewart, and his tone left no doubt that the call was very much in the urgent category.

'John,' he said without preamble, 'is it true you've decided to sue MI6?'

'No, of course not,' I said, 'we looked at that option and ruled it out completely. I would never change my mind without consulting you.'

Alastair sounded relieved. 'I thought not but the story has just broken on UpstairsBackstairs. And, of course, everyone is picking it up. You're supposed to have decided to sue MI6 for wrongful dismissal and are seeking damages for libel over the Rome allegations.'

'That's total nonsense,' I said, 'are there any clues who launched it?'

'No, they're quoting 'intelligence sources'.

'Let me look into it. I'll call you back.'

I closed off the call and told Chunk what had happened. His response was to hand me a glass of champagne.

'I'd better not,' I said. 'Looks like time for a clear head.'

I switched on my regular cell-phone and saw that I had been deluged with calls from virtually every media outlet in England, as well as a few from the States.

I borrowed Chunk's iPad, logged onto the Internet and went straight to UpstairsBackstairs.

U-B, as it was commonly known, was a rogue news agency which prided itself on printing any information that came its way. It never guaranteed the truth of any of it. It simply printed the leak, or rumour or gossip and invited its readers - and there were millions of them - to post anything they thought they knew about it. Despite making no claims to underwrite its stories, U-B gave a spurious air of veracity to them by writing tabloid headlines and doing agency-style re-writes to summarise the latest information coming in. Its followers relished the style and many of them loved to post whatever would make the most mischief. The items then triggered Twitter storms and threads on every other social media outlet.

The first headline read :

'Ex-spy hero John Saxon planning to sue his former employers. MI6 accused of corruption and libel. High Court action planned.'

The immediate follow-up was a distorted account of what had actually happened.

'Four years ago, while he was an MI6 intelligence officer, John Saxon began investigating corruption in his own service and in the CIA. He claims an attempt was made in Rome to stop the investigation by hatching a scheme to discredit him. In the course of this, Saxon says, his wife was killed and he was accused of murdering a young Italian officer who had been having an affair with her. Saxon claims a deal was struck with MI6 to smooth everything over but his employers are reneging on promises they made and Saxon his going for substantial damages.'

'Someone is being very devious,' Chunk said, as he read over my shoulder. 'This is clever stuff.'

It was indeed a very carefully crafted travesty. The only true line was that I had been investigating corruption and there had been a scheme to discredit me. The Italian officer had not been having an affair with my wife and his death had been an accident. The deal with MI6 which had prevented my arrest on trumped-up charges had not been to 'smooth things over' but to save MI6 from having to admit they had known the murder charge was phoney but they had gone along with it to please Washington.

The last thing I wanted was to have the whole business raked up again, especially with an organisation as treacherous and amoral as UpstairsBackstairs as the platform.

'You're assuming Vossler is behind this?' Chunk said.

I nodded. 'Aren't you?'

I quickly called Birdy in Weymouth. They had all seen the news and were all receiving and ignoring calls, but there had been no specific developments.

I asked if Kate was OK and was assured she was busy and well-guarded.

I closed the call and saw that Chunk had gone to answer the door bell. It was a courier with a letter for me. It was from MI6 cancelling my appointment and advising me that someone would be in touch 'in due course'.

'Did you tell anyone I was here?' I asked Chunk.

'No.'

'So, I'm being watched.'

'Of course. What did you expect?'

'Not any of this, that's for sure,' I said.

'So what do you plan to do?' Chunk looked concerned.

'I think it's time for a serious word with the Queen of the MI6 labyrinth, Virginia Walsh,' I said.

4

For someone who was supposed to be in the security business, Virginia Walsh had always been pretty cavalier about her own safety. At heart, she was a bureaucrat. She believed that the nasty stuff that crossed her desk every day happened to other people in lands far away. It took me less than ten minutes to break into her house and I was fairly confident that no one had seen me. To be fair, I wasn't exactly unprepared. Invading Virginia's private sanctum was something I had planned very carefully over many months. During the period when I had been officially 'in disgrace' I had made various contingency plans to deal with emergencies. Getting into her house was one of them, and I had done it before.

Virginia lived in St John's Wood, in a millionaire's row mansion that had been paid for mainly by her shady tax accountant husband. Her neighbours were all safely secluded behind high walls and thick, elegant hedges, which made it fairly easy to get close. The grounds at the back of the house belonged to St John's Wood Church. There were a few mourners in the graveyard and some families strolling or playing in the grassy area around it but no-one paid me any attention.

The burglar alarm could have been a challenge but I had long since done my homework. The Walsh's had installed an expensive, sophisticated model, but that had been some time ago and they hadn't bothered to upgrade to the latest technology. From my operational days, I had kept an electronic device which would deal with it. I retrieved that from my Covent Garden flat and was happy to gamble that she wouldn't have bothered to make any changes to the system. Luckily, I was right.

I broke in just before 6 o'clock in the evening. Virginia hadn't got home and I made a quick check to make sure there was no one else in the house. Then I began to look around, casually at first, but once I started, I slipped into old habits and began a systematic search.

The downstairs rooms were much as I had remembered them, elegant, stylish and fairly soulless. The ornaments were expensive and decorative but very impersonal with no suggestion of any attempt at real homemaking. There was one photograph of Virginia with her husband, a posed shot taken in what appeared to be someone else's garden. The surroundings were informal but both had put on formal smiles and appropriate postures.

The lounge had obviously been decorated for entertaining rather than family living. The French windows gave onto a walled garden which I knew already was carefully tended but very little used.

One look at the kitchen confirmed that Virginia was no cook. It contained every possible implement and gadget but no sign of wear and tear. There were no growing herbs and the fridge contained several expensively- packaged ready-meals designed for the microwave. I thought suddenly of my late wife, Sarah, who had been a superb cook. She had once pointed out that some of the greatest meals we had ever eaten in friends' houses in France had come from ovens with two settings, on and off, controlled by a switch you could barely operate for the grease.

Whenever I was dealing with Virginia, I usually ended up thinking about Sarah. She had been raped and killed in the shambles that had got me unjustly kicked out of MI6. In the aftermath, she had been painted as a slut and a whore. Virginia knew that was a total lie but had done nothing to defend her or me. The name of the game had been 'let's not upset Washington,' and what Washington wanted was to cover for Ray Vossler. Virginia had known how corrupt he was. She knew why I had been tracking him and how he had rigged the whole scenario to put a stop to my investigations yet she had still orchestrated my departure under an apparent cloud, forcing me to take a new identity and a new career in the BBC. Though Vossler was now in jail and I was being officially rehabilitated, I found it hard to forgive her.

I went upstairs to continue the search not expecting any real surprises and I wasn't ready for what I found in the first room. It was completely given over to embroidery! Once a bedroom, the room had been cleared to make space for rows of display cabinets containing exquisitely worked pieces of various sizes and designs. There was a comfortable armchair, surrounded by three tables with multiple shelves, which formed a rather elegant kind of workbench. It was an interest I had never suspected in all the years I had known Virginia, revealing a softer, artistic side which seemed alien to her nature.

From there, I went into the master bedroom and it was immediately obvious that Virginia was occupying it alone. There was a double wardrobe but one side of it – clearly her husband's – was empty except for a solitary pair of shoes and a new, virtually unworn tracksuit. Virginia's side contained several of her trademark dark suits and a collection of elegant formal dresses, suitable for official cocktail parties, together with a couple of kaftans she probably used for lounging around the house.

In the adjacent cabinet, there were two drawers which revealed a slightly surprising taste for Gucci and Victoria's Secret underwear. There was some jewellery in an unlocked box but it was not particularly stylish or expensive and I presumed she must have some better stuff in the wall safe.

I was careful to leave both rooms without any sign of disturbance and looked around for a suitable hiding place to wait for Virginia. I intended our meeting to give her a shock. I wanted her to know how vulnerable she was and that if she was going to go to war with me I could play as dirty as she could.

I waited for about half an hour then heard someone unlocking the front door. No car had come into the driveway and I assumed she'd been dropped outside by an official vehicle. I took a quick look to make sure no one was with her, then went back into a small annexe to one of the spare bedrooms. Virginia pottered about downstairs for about ten minutes then came up to the master bedroom, presumably to change out of her work clothes. I had guessed right and could hear sounds of undressing and drawers and cupboards being opened. I gave her a reasonable time then opened the master bedroom door, not particularly caring whether she was decent or not.

I got the effect I wanted. Virginia looked absolutely stunned. She had changed into the blue caftan with an oriental design that I had seen earlier. She stood for a moment, completely unable to speak, then she made a move towards her handbag which was on a chair beside the bed. I stepped across quickly and blocked her path.

'No mobiles, no alarms, Virginia. Don't worry, I just want to talk.'

Then she found her voice.

'You bastard,' she shrieked. 'Bastard, bastard, bastard.'

The invective built from there. The cursing varied from crude to imaginative and went on for the best part of a minute. I waited for a pause, then said calmly. 'It's alright Virginia. I'm not here to harm you and I haven't done any damage to your lovely home.'

'I don't give a shit about my house,' she yelled. 'It's my career you're damaging. I have been battling on your behalf for the past two weeks. I've been pleading your case with anyone who would listen. I've put my reputation on the line for you, and I've just spent two hours fending off people who said I should have known you would fucking-well sue us.'

'I'm not going to sue anyone,' I said calmly. 'Why don't we go downstairs and have a quiet discussion. Then I'll leave you in peace.'

Virginia didn't move immediately but I went to the door and she reluctantly followed. We went down into the lounge and I thought for a moment she was going to offer me a drink, in some kind of hospitality reflex. She stopped short and stood with her back to French windows, waiting for me to begin.

I sat down and indicated the sofa opposite.

'This a chat not a confrontation,' I said and waited until she sat down.

'First let's be clear. I am not going to sue. I considered it, of course I did, but at no point did I decide to pursue the idea.'

'They won't believe you.'

'Perhaps not, but they will believe Sir Alastair. He's a personal friend of the Chief, but that aside, everyone in the inner circle, including you, knows Alastair would never tell an outright lie. He might refuse to answer, if a disclosure compromised a client, but if he says plainly and straightforwardly, as he will, that I've never contemplated suing, he will be believed.'

Virginia didn't look reassured.

'So how do you explain all this?'

'For god's sake, Virginia, you know what UpstairsBackstairs is like. They'll print any rumour just for the hell of it.'

'Maybe, but this afternoon I had a call from one of the best investigative journalists in the world.'

'Who?'

'Sheila Cayman of the *New York Times*. She said she knew you were going to sue and she's flying to London to develop the story. Those were her exact words. 'develop the story'. Are you saying she didn't get that from you?'

'She most certainly didn't,' I said. 'Whatever she's got, she didn't get it from me. I don't even know her.'

'Well she certainly didn't get anything from me,' Virginia said sharply.

'You said you've been defending me,' I said, 'could the material have come from those who are against me?'

'That's simply not possible. Only the Chief, the head of Middle East Operations and myself have had access to your file. You will have to take my word that none of us approached Cayman or any other journalists.'

'I believe you,' I said, 'we both know perfectly well who is behind all this. I came here to warn you that it's important for you to stand by me.'

I made certain that she would notice my change of tone. My words were friendly but my eyes were not.

'What more do you want from me. I am standing by you. We're already collaborating with your legal team. We've handed over enough material to Sir Alastair to ensure that you can't possibly be extradited to Italy. We have an assurance from the Italian Ministry of the Interior that they accept that you were falsely accused.'

'Virginia, I said, 'let's drop the bullshit. You've been doing the absolute minimum you think you can get away with. You've been playing at defending me. So far, I've gone along with all your bureaucratic nonsense – how you acted on the 'best information you had at the time', mistakes were made, lessons have been learned, all that crap.

'You knew exactly what went on in Rome, as it was happening. You had all the information you needed to clear my name, all along. Instead, you hung me out to dry, partly to protect your own miserable career and partly, I admit, to protect what you saw as the interests of the Service.'

'That's water under the bridge.'

'Not any more. This nonsense on UpstairsBackstairs isn't about stopping me repairing my relations with MI6 by pretending I'm planning to sue. This is the Vosslers preparing to re-write history to save the miserable skin of brother Ray. They're going to deny I was investigating his corruption. They're going to start all over again about how I was a loose cannon in Rome, who went off the rails because my wife was a whore who was having affairs.'

Virginia stared ahead of her as if frozen to her chair, knowing what was coming next.

'What I came to tell you is that this time, you are going to really defend me. You have to be ready to come clean about the whole business, every detail: what I was doing in Rome, who I was investigating for corruption, why they tried to shut me down.'

I paused for just a moment then added, 'and exactly how you fucked my career in order to please Washington.'

'That's not possible.'

'It's going to have to be possible.'

'Or what?'

'Or I will break you. And I'll make sure the world knows the whole story whatever the consequences for me or MI6. I won't accept any fudges. There won't be any deals or bureaucratic horseshit. Do we understand each other?'

Virginia sighed.

'Yes. I understand. I'll do my best.'

'Yes, Virginia, you will, and this time it had better do the job.'

5

The next morning I flew back to Weymouth and Birdy met me at the air strip. 'Brace yourself,' he said 'your ex-girlfriend Marie-Hélène has turned up. She's been locked in with Kate for the last hour.' He grinned. 'And there's something else. You're so popular with the media that the boat's under siege!'

On the drive into town, Birdy gave me the full story. Marie had turned up completely unannounced and asked to see me. When she learned I was in London, she asked to see Kate and the two had been together in her cabin – our cabin – ever since.

Most of the network that arrived and had gathered on board the *Jessica*, the other boat we had chartered to accommodate them. I gathered they were anticipating a full-blown catfight. Bets were being taken and the odds were currently about even.

'If you'd asked me before I'd have put my money on Kate, no question,' Birdy said, 'but now I've seen Marie I'm not so sure.'

I could see the smile in his eyes and I knew that neither he nor the rest of the network would take this very seriously. A current and a past girlfriend in conflict was going to be the subject of a lot of ribbing.

On the press build-up, Birdy sounded more serious.

'It's pretty bad. The marina is blocked in every direction.'

'The gang got through all right?'

'Tim and Rachel came before it got too bad. Someone tried to block Lottery when he arrived with his new girlfriend, Clara. Lottery wouldn't say anything but the hack got nasty. Big mistake. He's going to need a dentist. The other hacks seem to have learned from that. Bob arrived just as I was leaving and we got the wheelchair through alright. You're going to be the big problem, but don't worry we've found a way in.'

'I don't understand it,' I said, 'my planning to sue MI6 just isn't that big a story.'

'Seems it is, old buddy. They're bloody everywhere. We've arranged for you to go in by boat.'

The marina had a system of landing stages which made it possible to get to any boat without a dinghy but as we approached I saw there were press people dotted around everywhere. Birdy drove me to the edge of the inner harbour where he had moored a small outboard near the adjacent bird sanctuary. We made our way quietly forward through the berthed cruisers and yachts without interference, but as we approached the stern of the *Jessica* a small motor boat pulled out and tried to block our path. A photographer was standing in the bow and the boat was being steered by what I took to be a journalist.

I prepared myself for a confrontation but there wasn't one. Lottery appeared on the *Jessica*'s transom with an eight-foot oar in his hand. He didn't speak and he wasn't brutal. He simply performed a gentle jousting movement, propelling the photographer into the water, complete with his camera equipment. Then he flicked the oar, as easily as if it had been made of balsa wood, and used it to gesture to the journalist that it was time for them to depart. Without even trying to get back on board, the photographer threw his sodden equipment into the boat and held onto the bow until the boat was well clear of us.

Lottery banged his oar smartly on the deck then held it upright in a mock naval salute and we climbed aboard.

'Tim has put me in charge of crowd control,' he said with a grin, 'but he won't let me use grenades.'

We went into the yacht's main saloon and found it full of old friends. The atmosphere reminded me of a military depot after leave, with everyone exchanging stories about what they've been doing, discussing accommodation details and chatting about what was coming up.

Tim and Rachel were off in one corner, deeply engaged in conversation, so I greeted Bob first. His handshake was warm but he looked tired and worried.

'I've got a lot to tell you,' he said, 'but I'd better leave it until all this has settled down. Right now all anyone is concerned about is what's happening with the two women.'

'What are the odds now?' Birdy asked.

Tim overheard and came over.

'Still evens I'd say.'

We shook hands and I congratulated him on his success with the training exercise. Lottery, who was nearby, laughed and said, 'be careful, John, that's a touchy subject.'

'Why?' I asked, 'I thought it was a big success.'

Lottery nodded. 'It was. That's the problem. Tim is the training hero of the hour but he's not sure he's ready for a life of grinding recruits into the ground.'

'It's not just recruits I'll be grinding,' Tim growled, 'you'd better bloody well watch out when you come in for your refreshers.'

'Right now, I'm more worried about Rachel,' Tim said, 'the big trial she was working on has collapsed on appeal, and she's seriously pissed off about it.'

I continued my tour of the saloon and found Jay sitting in the corner fiddling with his artificial foot.

'It's a new one,' he explained, 'I've just come back from the rehab centre at Haverly. It's a lot better than the old one but it's going to take some time to bed in.'

'The only one without problems is Lottery,' Birdy said.

'I wish,' Lottery grunted, 'that's my problem over there.' He pointed to an attractive, dark-haired young woman who had just joined the group. 'That's Clara. She's supposed to be my new girlfriend but if this goes on it's not going to last out the week. I promised her a holiday away from the army and all I've done so far is beat up journalists and run a book on your love life.'

He glanced over my shoulder. 'Looks as though we're going to find out who's going to make the money.'

Kate and Marie had come onto the deck of the *Jurassic Star* and were coming across the gangway which linked the two boats.

I knew straight away that everyone had got it wrong. Neither was smiling but both looked completely at ease though in quite different ways. The contrast between them was striking. Kate was in her usual sailing pants and an orange and black Ocean Reports sweatshirt. Marie looked almost formal, in a plain blue sun dress which hid her curves more discreetly than usual – she could have been on holiday with the smart set or heading for a company meeting.

Tim made way for them to settle at the bow end of the saloon and we all waited expectantly.

'I'm sorry to disappoint you,' Kate began, 'there's been no catfight. Not a single hair has been pulled. This is not a tug of love. We waited for John to arrive because he's directly concerned,' she gave me a brief but friendly smile, 'but so are you all. Marie has come to help us. I'll let her introduce herself and tell you all why she's here.'

She sat down and left Marie to address the group. Everyone watched with stunned attention as she took the floor.

'Some background first,' Marie began. 'My name is Marie Cassia. I'm a lawyer – what you would call a barrister – practising in Paris. John knows already that I've just left the family firm and I'm taking a short career break before setting up my own practice.'

Marie looked across at me. 'I must make it clear that John has never told me anything about your affairs. Before your great confrontation with Ray Vossler and his associates, I knew him as John Cartwright, a harmless,' she smiled, 'but very charming BBC editor. Our affair ended some time ago but I have been following your adventures in the press and social media.' She smiled across at Cronin. 'Apart from John the only one of you I know personally is Bob. We have faced each other across the bridge table, in international competitions.'

I was surprised but I shouldn't have been. I knew that Marie had been part of the French national bridge team and it was natural that she would have come across Bob at some time in her playing career.

'The woman who is going to be my one of my new London law associates knew of my interest,' Marie went on, 'and she called me with some information that I believe will be very important to you.

'She has discovered that Vossler has hired a London PR company to run a dirty tricks campaign against you. They intend to target you all individually, then attack you as a group and it's not just any PR company, it's a particularly sleazy operation run by woman you may have heard of, Maxine Herald.'

Rachel gave a little sigh. 'Wonderful,' she said, 'one of her pet hates is the police, and the Met in particular.'

'I'm sure you all know that Maxine Herald is completely without scruples and she's masterly at manipulating social networking, particularly websites like UpstairsBackstairs. She's certainly behind the leak about John wanting to sue MI6. But according to my associate there's a great deal more to come. If you take a moment to think about it, you'll realise that the media scrum out there is far bigger than is justified by the suing rumour.'

'The people who are making a nuisance of themselves on the quayside are not Sports journalists,' Kate interrupted. 'They're mostly tabloid hacks. Since talking to Marie, I've been in touch with some former BBC colleagues and apparently the word is out that a really big story is about to break here in Weymouth. No one knows yet what it is but the tabloids have been told that it's worth their while to send people down here.'

'What we don't know yet,' Marie resumed, 'is how Ray Vossler is going to orchestrate this campaign from prison.'

Bob Cronin raised his arm then edged his wheelchair to the front of the group.

'If I could say a few words here,' he said, 'I think I can give you the bigger picture. It's not Ray Vossler who is behind this, it's the whole Vossler group.'

Marie helped Bob manoeuvre his chair to a position where everyone could see him then she sat down on the bench beside Kate.

'This is what I came to Weymouth to talk to you all about,' he said. 'I didn't know about Maxine Herald but that fits in exactly with what I've heard from my sources in Washington. What we're dealing with here is a campaign by the whole Vossler Group and all the allies they can muster, and believe me that's a lot of firepower.'

He eased himself forward in his wheelchair.

'About ten days ago, the Vossler group held a meeting at their mansion outside Washington, DC. It's taken me a while, but I've managed to get a pretty good account of what went on. None of it is good news.'

'Do we know who was there?' I asked.

'All the usual suspects. Ivan and Mark Vossler. Most of the Vossler board. In fact, all of the senior figures. But apart from the brothers, the most important ones were the Finance director, Leo Krantz and the Communications director, Alan Brody.'

'Do they really matter?' I said. 'I thought Ivan and Mark called the shots.'

'I'll get to that,' Bob said, 'what you have to grasp is this was a day-long conclave, attended by everyone who matters. It was decision day and the only issue on the table was: what were they going to do about Ray Vossler?

They discussed two options. The first was to hang him out to dry. Simply disown him and cut him loose, distance the Group from everything he's done.'

'And the second option was to rally round and save him,' Tim prompted.

'Exactly.'

'I'm surprised there was even a debate,' I said. 'There's no love lost between Ray and his two brothers. They have always treated Ray as a necessary evil.'

'That's exactly right,' Cronin said. 'Ivan and Mark were all set to say 'fuck him'. They simply wanted to circle the wagons and leave Ray on the outside.'

'So what happened?' Kate asked.

'The Finance and PR directors weighed in and said that wouldn't work. Leo Krantz argued that Ray was simply too valuable to cut loose. He said Ray's expertise and contacts were irreplaceable. That didn't go down too well but Krantz insisted it was very unlikely the group's income could be increased or even maintained at its present level without Ray and that got their attention.'

Cronin paused. 'I'm not sure whether Krantz alone could have swayed the meeting but Brody, the PR man, clinched the decision. My source told me everyone was surprised at how strongly Brody came out. Apparently he was known pretty much as an ass-licker who always took care to keep on the right side of Ivan and Mark. But this time, he told the brothers they were living in dreamland. He said that if Ray was convicted of terrorist offences the group would never recover. Brody said the group would never convince even the cosiest of insider journalists that the brothers hadn't known what Ray was up to.'

Cronin eased himself upright in his wheelchair and I could see he was getting uncomfortable.

'You can imagine the row that broke out. Ivan and Mark aren't used to being talked to like that but apparently Brody stood his ground. He said the only way the group could survive was to put on a bold face, rally to Ray's defence and find some way to get him acquitted. He said that if they couldn't manage that and Ray was convicted, then the group should still continue to maintain that he'd been railroaded, and that the Brits were persecuting him to get at the Americans.'

It was Birdy who put the question we all wanted to ask.

'So how did it end?'

'Sadly for us, it ended with an agreement that they would all go away and draft contributions to a 'Save Ray' campaign. They met again two days ago and I'm waiting for a full report from my sources. But judging by what Marie has said and the rumours about John suing MI6, plus what happened to Kate, we can assume the campaign has already begun.'

He turned to Kate 'I know you're going to hate me for saying this but you're going to have to let these guys monitor you for a while.'

To my surprise, Kate didn't explode. Instead, she stood up and said calmly, 'thanks for that, Bob, it makes sense.'

'Our good news is that Marie has kindly offered to assist us,' she said. 'She's going to stay in Weymouth for a few days and help us deal with the social networking attacks and with the media generally. She knows how busy I will be. Jay has a lot of expertise in this area as well, I know, and I'm going to ask him to work with Marie and organise our defences as best they can.'

She smiled at the group. 'I hope you don't mind my taking over like this but this is Ocean Reports' show and I'm responsible for keeping it on the road – or rather on the water.'

'How can we keep in touch with Marie,' Tim asked, 'where are you staying?'

Kate smiled again, first towards the group and then directly at me.

'I've made room for Marie on board the *Jurassic Star*. She's going to have the second cabin.'

6

My first impulse was to get Kate alone and ask her what the hell she thought she was playing at, but before I got the chance Inspector Frampton arrived. He had with him a giant of a man who looked much more like a sailor than a policeman. He was about 20 years old and heavily muscled with the kind of dark shadowy tan that didn't come from sunbathing. Frampton showed his ID to the group then introduced him as Matt Lano.

'Matt is about to become a police cadet,' Frampton said, 'but at the moment he spends most of his time helping his father on board the family trawler. I'll explain in a minute why I've brought him here.'

Frampton gestured vaguely behind him.

'It's getting pretty chaotic out there,' he said, 'I'm trying to restore some kind of order but it's not easy. The marina is bringing in extra security and I'm assigning as many men as I can, but I've been trying to work out some kind of a deal with the journalists.

'I know you're not going to like this, but they want a press conference. A simple statement won't buy them off.'

'I'm willing to do that,' I said, 'but I need at least an hour to prepare.'

'That's fine,' Frampton said, 'but it won't be enough. They want all of you to take part in a press conference.'

'Why would they want all of us?' I asked, 'the story is whether or not I'm planning to sue MI6.'

'That may well be, but they still want all of you. They want to know why you are gathered here, what you're all actually doing in Weymouth.'

'We're here for a party,' Tim said, 'but you'd never guess it from the way things are going.'

'So just tell them that. Make it convincing and I'm sure they'll be happy. You know how to do it. I saw the press conference you gave after the set-to in London. It passed off superbly.'

'Well, for a start they don't need me,' Kate said, 'I've got work to do.'

Frampton looked apologetic. 'I'm sorry but they insisted. They want everyone.'

'Well they can bloody well go on wanting!'

'Look,' Frampton said, 'I need your help on this. They're a flaming nuisance and they're not going to go away unless we throw them some kind of bone. Right now, this place is under siege. I have no doubt whatever that you lot are capable of fighting your way out, however many of them there are, but I don't want a riot on my hands in the middle of the Olympic Games.'

He looked directly at Kate. 'I do understand that you are here to cover the Games and I want to help you do that in any way I can. But in return, please help me by doing this one press conference.'

He smiled suddenly, 'and in return I will lend you Bouncer for a week.'

He turned to the young man beside him. 'We call him Bouncer because that's what he does at the weekends to get a bit of extra money when his Dad lets him off the boat.'

He smiled at Kate. 'I've gathered how much you hate being protected but we have to face realities. Every time you go to the press centre you're going to be bothered by somebody. I could arrange for one of your so-called network to be accredited and accompany you everywhere, but they'd only be asked questions as well, making it even worse. If you have Bouncer with you, you'll find life a great deal easier. He understands the problem and he won't bother you in any way. More importantly, I trust him to keep the peace without causing a ruckus. That's why I've brought him along. Do we have a deal?'

'I guess I don't really have a choice,' Kate said, 'so welcome aboard, Bouncer.' She smiled suddenly, 'at least, you know more about boats than this lot.'

Frampton looked relieved. 'Right,' he said, 'I'll arrange a press conference for two hours' time, in Saint Xavier's Hall on the other side of the harbour. Is that enough time for you to prepare?'

'That'll be fine,' I said, 'and thanks for your help.'

When Frampton had gone, I still couldn't find the opportunity to get Kate alone. Bob's partner, Leslie, arrived to take him to the hotel and we had a few quick words.

Usually, Leslie was seriously hostile to me and to the other members of the network. He was convinced that Bob was damaging his health by becoming involved in the stresses of intelligence work instead of helping run their bridge school in Norfolk. When he was defending Bob from what he saw as the intrusion of his intelligence past, he could be quite vicious and I didn't want a fight over Bob's health on top of everything else. I was expecting Leslie to start straight in on how we were endangering his partner yet again. Instead he gave me a friendly handshake and a rueful smile.

'Will the bridge school be OK while you're away?' I asked.

'We've closed it for a while. But don't worry, I'm not going to bite your head off.'

He gave Bob an affectionate look.

'That doesn't mean the stupid fool is any better, in fact if anything he's a bit worse, but I've given up the fight. The truth is he likes all this intelligence shit a lot better than he likes running a bridge school. He's come to life since this whole business began. We've closed the school for the rest of the summer, so he can do what he can to help.'

'I'm sorry,' I said, 'I didn't want all this to disrupt your lives that much.' Bob patted Leslie's arm.

'We'll both survive just fine. As soon as we get the chance I'll give Leslie his bridge fix. We'll play a few high-stakes matches to keep him quiet.'

Kate had gone across to the *Jurassic Star* with Marie and once Marie was settled in her cabin, I planned to confront Kate and find out what the hell she thought she doing, having Marie sleeping on board. But before I could follow them, Kate came storming back across the gang plank carrying an open laptop.

'For Christ's sake, look at this,' she shouted.

On the screen there was a page of UpstairsBackstairs. The headline read. **'Yachtie Kate sued for damage to speedboat.'**

Directly underneath, there was a photograph of the little red speedboat that Kate had used to rescue me from *HMS Belfast* when my true identity had first been exposed at the BBC.

The first part of the account was roughly accurate. It described how I had been working at the BBC under the fake identity of John Cartwright when I had been accidentally discovered by Ray Vossler. I had got into a furious fight with Vossler's bodyguard, Ali Omar. To try to avoid my identity from being revealed, I had run to the museum ship, *HMS Belfast*, which was moored on the Thames, where I had friends I thought could hide me. But I had been followed and cornered there and had got away only because Kate had driven a speedboat along the river to ensure my escape.

Below, however, was another photo showing the speedboat with a badly damaged hull. The caption below read: **'Beware women drivers!'** It went on to say that Kate had subsequently steered the boat into a piling at a nearby dock and had hidden it to prevent the boatyard from finding out. The owners had now found it and were said to be furious. A supposed spokesman for the yard was quoted as saying that the owners would have been more understanding if Kate had admitted the accident in the first place, but they were now planning to insist on compensation for the damage. There were more pictures of the boat in close-up which showed a gash in the hull and extensive scratching and denting just above the waterline.

Marie had obviously heard Kate's shout and came across the gangplank after her. She had already changed into something like sailing gear, but even in her new relaxed mode, she still looked more like a sponsor than a yachtswoman.

She looked at the laptop screen, saw what the situation was and immediately took over. I had never really seen Marie at work and I was very impressed. I stood beside her and we both read over Kate's shoulder.

I had to admit the story was both subtle and damning. There was no direct interview with the owner of the boatyard. It was all attributed to 'boatyard sources' but it was written in a way that suggested that the owner, or someone very close to him, had been recounting the story in detail.

It was being treated as a breaking story and Marie said quickly, 'there's only about an hour before we have to leave for the press conference. I'll deal with the Kate story, you'd better prepare a statement about you not suing MI6.'

I went with them back on board the *Jurassic Star*, found my own laptop and we started work. In fact, I already had in my head what I planned to say and as I wrote, I listened, fascinated, to the way Marie was dealing with Kate.

First she asked Kate how she had come to rescue me at all.

Kate explained that after my fight in the World Service newsroom I had fled, but she had noticed that Vossler had immediately made a call on his mobile phone. From the newsroom window she had seen Vossler's driver parked in the street below, taking a call. She then saw me getting into a taxi with Vossler's driver following. She had rushed down and managed to follow them, in her own car. Once she realised I had taken refuge on board *HMS Belfast* and was trapped, she had called a friend in a nearby boatyard and asked if she could borrow the speedboat.

Marie listened carefully then said, 'now tell me exactly what happened after the rescue.'

Kate described how we had gone into hiding on board a luxury cruiser in St Katherine's Dock, having hidden the speedboat nearby. Later, she had called the same friend. He had collected the boat and taken it safely back to the original boatyard.

'Are you quite sure it was taken back safely?' Marie asked.

Kate didn't hesitate. 'I'm absolutely sure. The guy who helped me is an old friend. We've sailed together. I trust him absolutely. I asked him if the boat had been returned without problems and he said it had gone absolutely smoothly. If he had damaged the boat, he would certainly have told me.'

'So we are saying that the boat was returned intact and the damage was done later, deliberately to cause trouble for you.'

'That has to be it.'

'Good,' Marie said, 'then let's start with a phone call to this man. See if you can reach him now.'

As Kate began to make the call, I saw her pause and stare again at the screen.

'What's happening now?' I asked, 'is there more?'

Kate didn't answer immediately then she said, 'no, it's this picture. That's not the same boat. It's similar. It's the same type and same colour but it's not the same one.'

'You're quite sure?'

'Definitely. The layout of the cockpit is different.'

'Good,' Marie said, 'so make the call.'

It took a while, but Kate did eventually manage to track down the friend who had lent her the boat. He hadn't been aware of the damage story and assured Kate that the speedboat she had used had been returned safely and was now out on hire to a family in Maidenhead.

He said the boatyard had three similar boats but he wasn't aware that any of them were damaged. Prompted by Marie, Kate asked him if he could log in and see if he recognised the damaged boat. After a few minutes' pause, he came back and said yes he did, and that boat was currently on hire to a corporate client.

The next problem was whether he could be asked to help without getting into trouble with the boatyard owners. Kate was reluctant to ask him but he assured her that it was in both their interests.

Within twenty minutes, he had emailed a signed statement saying that he had helped Kate by loaning her the boat, that it had been returned safely, and that he had later told the boat yard owners what he had done. He certified that there was no damage to the boat and that the one being photographed on the Internet was a different craft.

Marie then helped Kate draft a statement which she would read at the press conference.

'That should be enough,' Marie said, 'just read the statement then answer any follow-up questions calmly,' she smiled, 'without getting too defensive.'

She turned to me, 'the same applies to you, John. Read your statement then answer as few questions as you can get away with, but make it convincing.'

'I'm ready,' I said, 'I know exactly what I want to say.'

'I'm sure you do,' Marie said, 'and that's what's worrying me slightly.'

'Why, what's wrong?'

'I'm not entirely sure,' Marie said, 'you've both got strong defences but Vossler has brought most of the London press corps down here. I have a feeling this is just a little too easy.'

7

'I can see the headline now,' Tim said, 'Crack SAS unit defended by Police Community Support Officers!'

It was a splendid moment! Inspector Frampton had arranged for a police van to drive along the quay and pick us up directly opposite the boat. There weren't many journalists about as most had left to secure places at the press conference, but a few had stayed behind and one photographer pushed his camera up against Tim's face. Before Tim could react, the leader of the Community Support Officers, a friendly, middle-aged woman with greying hair called Hazel, put herself between them and told the photographer in no uncertain terms to back off. Her fierceness surprised all of us and the photographer retreated without argument.

As we were getting into the van, we heard Hazel say, 'don't worry we'll take good care of you.'

The church hall where the press conference was being held was some way from harbour. We were driven to the back entrance and shown into a kind of ante-room which served as a kitchen and storage area. We had agreed that Frampton should remain in charge and he showed himself surprisingly efficient. He had insisted that all the journalists sign in and he gave us a list of names together with their organisations.

Kate and I scanned it quickly and we saw straightaway that there were a lot of unfamiliar names. About two thirds of the hundred or so people on the list worked for conventional media organisations and we knew most of them either well or through casual contact. The remaining third had listed themselves as bloggers or as working for websites that neither of us were familiar with. The make-up of the list made me very suspicious and my fears were confirmed as soon as we got into the main hall. Marie and Jay waited in the ante-room with their laptops to monitor any breaking news and social network reaction and Frampton led the rest of us out to the fray.

The main hall was packed. In a mildly surreal touch, the room was decorated with children's drawings, mostly coloured stick figures intended to illustrate Weymouth's welcome to the Olympic sailors.

As soon as we filed out of the ante-room, cameras started clicking and flashing into our faces. Frampton sat in the centre; Kate and I sat either side; Birdy and Tim took the outside positions with Lottery on the end, near the ante-room door.

The BBC crew had secured a place right in the front of a good three rows of cameramen and photographers, some of whom were still jostling for position. Both Kate and I knew the BBC reporter, Caroline Smallwood, very well and she gave us a friendly wave as we came in. Her cameraman, Josh Wilkins, was someone I knew only slightly but his smile was also welcoming.

It began in a fairly orderly manner. Frampton said a few words of introduction, thanking everyone for coming and explaining that this would be the only opportunity to meet members of the network. After this, he said, the network would be strictly off limits and unavailable either for interviews or questioning.

I spoke next and did my best to appear genial and relaxed. I said that all the members of what had become known as the Saxon Network were here for a holiday, except Kate, who was in Weymouth to cover the Olympic Games for a syndicate of American magazines. I explained that we were here to party and enjoy the Games and for no other reason. I confirmed what Frampton had said: that we would answer any questions anyone had, but after that, there would be no more contact with the press as we would be concentrating on enjoying the sailing.

Next, I read a short statement saying that there was absolutely no truth in rumours that I was planning to sue my former employers MI6.

I said that my solicitor, Sir Alastair Stewart, would be having a meeting very shortly with senior officials of MI6, and there would be a joint statement afterwards with both sides confirming that this was the case.

As I was speaking, I scanned the room carefully. As always, the mainstream journalists had divided into two distinct packs, those I regarded as the serious journalists, and the ones I thought of as the tabloid hooligans. The unfamiliar third group had mostly gathered at the back and seem to have formed a kind of square. Most of those in the room had either smartphones or tablets and many started to tweet as soon as I began speaking, but I noticed the group at the back were watching their screens intently rather than sending messages. They were paying only scant attention to what I was saying and I prepared myself for trouble.

I let the BBC have the first question and Caroline asked if I had ever considered suing MI6. I said that my solicitor had asked me, as a matter of routine, but I had ruled it out from the outset and it was never an issue.

'Is that because you wanted to protect your wife's reputation?' a woman yelled from the back.

'No, certainly not', I said, 'my wife's reputation was never in question at any point.'

'But if you did sue, it would come out in court that she was having an affair with the Italian officer you killed,' the same woman shouted.

'Let's get the facts absolutely correct, they have been widely misconstrued from the outset,' I said, 'my wife had no affair with the Italian lieutenant. His death was accidental. I was trying to save my wife when the lieutenant tried to stop me. I punched him and he fell and hit his head on the curb.'

'Did you decide not to sue because MI6 agreed to go along with this version of events?' another questioner shouted.

'There you go again. This is not a version of events. It is the simple truth,' I replied.

'But your wife was having an affair with the man who eventually killed her.' This was another shout from the back, this time from a different woman.

'I suggest you change your choice of media,' I said, 'I repeat, my wife was not having an affair with anyone. As you well know, the man who killed her, Ali Omar, is a known terrorist and a vicious individual, who is currently in jail in London. He harassed her very severely. She resisted, then tried to escape. Omar chased her in a jeep and ran her down. The courts still have to decide whether it was an accident or deliberate.'

At this point Frampton intervened.

'I think it's time we moved on,' he said, 'Mr Saxon has answered the question. He has made it quite clear that he is not planning to sue MI6. I think it's Kate's turn to say a few words. She also has a statement to read.'

There were several shouts of protest. Frampton ignored them and indicated to Kate that she should begin her statement. I was growing more and more uneasy. I'd been to enough press conferences to know that I was still a target. It was obvious that whether or not I was going to sue MI6 was not the main agenda, nor were the tabloid hacks interested in details of what had really happened in Rome. For them, that was history. I was sure they had something much more current on their minds and I could sense a trap was about to be sprung. I couldn't figure out what it was but I didn't have to wait long.

Kate positioned her microphone and began to read the statement she had worked out with Marie, proving beyond doubt that she had not damaged any speedboat. She was allowed to finish without interruptions but it was clear the journalists in the room couldn't care less. That wasn't why they were there.

A woman from the square at the back opened the attack, under cover of a simple enquiry.

'Can you tell us, Kate, when your next sailing expedition will be?'

'Nothing is set exactly. The details are still being worked out.'

'Is it true that your main sponsor is going to be Ocean Reports?'

Kate glanced across at me. I knew the answer was yes but I also knew Kate had been waiting for the right moment to tell me. The subject of her sailing plans and our future relationship was one where we both danced on eggshells.

Kate hesitated for a moment then said calmly, 'nothing is settled yet, but yes, Ocean Reports is considering sponsoring me.'

Then the trap was sprung.

'Do they know about your plans to marry John Saxon?'

Kate looked stunned. She glanced quickly at me then said, 'I have no plans to marry John.'

'But you are living with him.'

'I am a single woman,' Kate snapped, 'and my relations with John have nothing to do with you, or anyone else in this room.'

I looked around. Everyone was looking down at the tablets and smartphones. Even reading upside down I could see several screens in the front row were displaying UpstairsBackstairs.

'There is a story running,' someone shouted, 'that you are keeping your wedding plans secret so as not to lose Ocean Reports' sponsorship. Can you comment on that?'

'That's absolute nonsense,' Kate said, 'it's pure fabrication.'

'So, you're saying Ocean Reports doesn't know about the wedding.'

'I've already told you. There are no wedding plans.'

The woman looked down at a tablet. 'So how do you explain the bidding war going on between *Hello!* magazine and *OK!* magazine for the rights to cover your wedding ceremony.'

'This is pure fantasy. There is no wedding to bid for.' She turned to me, 'John, can you take over?'

'Kate is right. We have absolutely no plans to marry.'

'Even though Kate is pregnant.'

'What did you say!'

'You mean she hasn't told you.'

'For God's sake,' Kate shouted, 'I have no plans to marry and I'm not pregnant.'

But there was no stopping them; the frenzy was in full force.

'Have you had an abortion?' someone shouted.

'No, of course not.'

'Would you consider an abortion if it meant losing your chance of a new expedition?'

'What kind of a question is that?' Kate said furiously. I shot her a warning glance. I was as angry as she was, but now was not the moment for us to lose our tempers.

'We have a quote here from a spokesman for Ocean Reports. They said they would never consider sponsoring anyone who had an abortion for the sake of undertaking an expedition.'

'Of course they wouldn't,' Kate said, 'the Publisher of Ocean Reports is a key figure in the American religious right.'

Kate was seriously rattled now but I knew we couldn't just break off the press conference.

'So you would know better than to ask?'

'Dammit, I have no reason to ask. I am not pregnant. I have not had an abortion. This is all pure nonsense.'

'I have something to say,' I said, as authoritatively as I could, indicating to Kate that she should sit down and stop responding. 'This whole circus is based on a tissue of lies running on UpstairsBackstairs, a website you all know to be absolutely and totally unreliable. You're responding to malicious mischief put out for the gullible and you all should know better than to pick up the kind of rubbish they put out.'

To my surprise, no one responded immediately. I'd expected the barrage to continue, but again, everyone was looking down at their tablets. When the questioning did continue, it took a tack I had never expected.

'John, is it true you're playing all this down to please Marie Cassia?' a woman shouted.

Before I could answer, the door to the anteroom opened and Jay came through and put an iPad in front of me. I read the UpstairsBackstairs headline.

'Ex-mistress flies in to plead with Saxon not to marry pregnant Kate.'

The story was as bad as it could get. It tied together all the lies and rumours that had been fuelling the press conference. It said that Marie was begging me to let Kate have an abortion so we didn't have to get married. The story was so outrageous that I didn't know how to begin the denial. As I was reading, dozens of questions were being shouted.

I looked up and saw the BBC reporter was trying to get my attention. In the hope of getting some sanity from her, I indicated that I was ready for his question.

'John is it true that Marie Cassia is in Weymouth?'

'I'll answer that question,' Kate interrupted, 'yes Marie is here. She's here is my friend and, as such, has been welcomed by the rest of the network.'

'Are you aware that John has just been with Marie in France?' someone else interrupted.

'Of course I am. They were there to attend the wedding of some old friends.'

As she spoke I looked down at the iPad. UpstairsBackstairs had started to run a series of pictures. The first one showed a general view of the Auberge. The second was a shot through our bedroom window, showing Marie dressed only in a thong, smiling at me as I lay on the bed.

'Kate did you know he was still shagging her?' someone yelled from the back.

But before Kate could answer, Jay started to go back into the anteroom and one of the photographers spotted Marie through the half open door.

'She's in there,' he shouted and made a dive for the door.

What came next happened so quickly that it was only unpicked properly later from the film and camera-phone footage. Lottery moved so swiftly that the photographer ran straight into him. There were no obvious punches, but the photographer let out a yelp of pain, dropped his camera and doubled up on the floor. Calmly, Lottery picked him up, and under the guise helping him after his fall, used him to block the oncoming rush of journalists. At the same time, Tim, Birdy and I moved in on either side of him, leaving room for Kate to slip out behind us.

We were all in a mood for a fight but it was Frampton who stopped it. In a powerful voice, he shouted 'anyone who takes a step forward will be arrested,' and there was no mistaking from his tone that he meant it.

Hazel and her fellow community support officers formed a quick barricade and we were bundled back into our police van.

'That went well then,' Tim said, but the joke fell flat. We all knew that we were on unfamiliar terrain and, in military terms, the Saxon Network had just been totally out-manoeuvred.

8

It was hard to see how things could get worse, but they did.

Back on board the *Jurassic Star*, I was ready for the inevitable row with Kate but it turned out not to really be a row. Kate didn't seem to care enough to get angry and we ended with a kind of sullen stand-off.

I began by saying as calmly as I could, 'I didn't have sex with Marie in France.'

Kate's answer was equally calm. 'I don't give a damn whether you did or not.'

'Kate, I really did not have sex with Marie,' I repeated, more slowly, emphasising each word.

'I told you I don't care.'

'Marie was just teasing me. She said being loyal to you was not very French and it was her duty to test my resolve. And I did pass.'

I was about to say, 'I told her I was in love with you,' but I held back, not sure if that would soothe Kate or upset her even more.

Kate misread my hesitation. 'So you were tempted. I'm not surprised with a body like that, compared to me and my scar.'

'Kate, look at me,' I said, 'think back to Gloucester. How many times did we make love? How many times did the scar make the slightest difference?'

On her last big sailing trip, a hawser had cut loose, whipping across her chest. The wound had left a scar from her breast to below her navel and a first round of plastic surgery had still left a very visible mark. She was planning to have more surgery but she was very sensitive about how her body looked.

I could see that no reassurances were going to work with her in this mood. We had barely spoken on the ride back from the press conference. I had been wedged between Lottery and Hazel, the Community Support Officer and, back at the quay, we had all been escorted into our separate boats before anyone could give chase.

Once on board, Marie had gone to the stern of the boat, deliberately leaving us alone.

'The teasing really was all on Marie's side,' I said.

'Really!'

'I shared a bed with her but absolutely nothing happened. I stayed the night because I couldn't fly the Tiger in the dark and I came back to Weymouth at first light.'

'And I suppose you didn't wake up curled around her like you always seem to end up doing.'

Kate was right of course. Several times in the night we had become entwined together but I had resisted and slipped away early to fly back to England before Marie could start testing me again.

'We couldn't insist on two rooms, the hotel was full,' I said, 'we had no option.'

I didn't mention Marie's scheming to bring us together. There was no point in making things worse, and it was true the hotel was overflowing.

'Well you have the option now. If you want to, you can change cabins and go aft right now.'

'Was that your idea in having Marie on board in the first place, to see if I would go cabin-hopping?'

Just for a second, Kate looked slightly sheepish, but she quickly recovered.

'No, it wasn't that,' she said wearily, 'I just thought you could have a daytime playmate to keep you out of my hair, so I could get on with my work. But as far as I'm concerned, you can cabin-hop, as you call it, any time you feel like it. You may as well. You won't get much action up here with my shoulder in its present state.'

'Kate, this is ridiculous,' I said, 'it wasn't a great idea to have Marie on board the *Jurassic Star* anyway. I'll arrange for her to go back to France. I'm sure she'll want to.'

'For Christ's sake, don't do that,' Kate said, 'you know what line UpstairsBackstairs will take: 'pregnant Kate kicks rival lover off boat to save her marriage to love rat John.'

I thought for a moment she was going to smile but she remained stone-faced.

'Are you sure you want her to stay? I said, 'UpstairsBackstairs will write what they want whether she goes or not.'

Kate didn't hesitate. 'We're not going to let that fucker Maxine Herald rule our lives. Marie stays where she is. We'll tough this one out.

You'd better go and see how she's taking it. If she's packing to leave, talk her out of it.'

I tried to lighten the mood.

'So permission to stay in the bow, Captain,' I said as gently as I could.

Kate nodded. 'Yeah okay, you may as well,' she said, but before I could say anything encouraging, she added quickly 'if you get too frustrated you can always change your mind and go aft.'

I knew there was no more to be done for the moment so I went down to Marie's cabin. She was sitting on the bunk and though she didn't literally have her head in her hands, she might as well have done. I had never seen her looking so shaken.

'This has been quite a lesson,' she said, 'I've had clients who've been destroyed by social media. Now I know what it feels like.'

'But you haven't been destroyed.'

It was a statement rather than a question but Marie went on speaking agitatedly.

'I've just had two phone calls. The first was from my father.'

'What did he say?'

'He was so angry I could barely make it out,' Marie said, 'but his main point was that it was a good job I'd left the firm. He is going to make sure that all the clients know that I won't be coming back and the break is permanent. Knowing him, I'm pretty sure he'll tell everyone this is the reason he fired me.'

'Surely he can't do that. It's some time since you left.'

'He'll find a way. Then I had my new partner on the phone.'

'She must have been sympathetic.'

'Sympathetic yes, but she thinks we ought to delay opening our new chambers until this blows over. And from the way she said 'blows over', it doesn't sound as though she has in mind for us to go into business at all. She hasn't resigned yet from the firm she's with and now I'm not sure she will.'

'We'll find a way of fighting back,' I said, 'I'll get everyone together for a debrief.'

There wasn't much conviction in my voice and Marie knew it.

'I presume Kate wants me off her boat,' she said.

'No, quite the opposite. She's quite determined. We have to tough it out. Those were her words.'

'Alright. I'll stay for the moment. Quite frankly, I'm not sure what to do.'

I was just about to start arranging a debrief on board the *Jessica* when I heard a door banging, followed by rapid footsteps through the saloon. Then the cabin door burst open and Kate strode in.

She was beside herself with anger and I thought at first she must have thought the situation over and changed her mind about wanting Marie to stay. Either that or she'd suddenly imagined she would find us making love behind her back, but when she spoke I knew that, in Kate's terms, it was something far worse.

'I've been canned,' she shouted. 'not in as many words but as good as. They didn't have the guts to come right out with it. They're sending in someone else, to lead the coverage while I'm dealing with the stress of my personal situation. How's that for a lovely weasel phrase? Not share the coverage, mind you, lead it. I'm to be allowed to assist as far as my situation allows!'

'Kate, I'm really sorry,' Marie began, but Kate interrupted sharply.

'It's not your fault. It's that witch Maxine Herald. John told me you were just kidding around in France. It's not important.'

Her indifference wasn't exactly promising but at least it was better than open warfare between the two women.

'Any chance you can get the sacking reversed?' I asked.

'Maybe. It still early morning in Massachusetts. Hard to say whether the big boss was consulted. Anyway, even if he wasn't, he'll probably go along with it. I'll try to speak to him later.'

'It's time for a team get-together,' I said, 'the press isn't going to leave us alone. We have to work out some strategy.'

I called Tim and within a quarter of an hour everyone was gathered in the saloon of the *Jessica*. While I was organising it, Kate took Marie aside. I couldn't hear what they were saying, but it didn't sound as though claws were out.

When we did all get together, it looked less like a briefing than a rugby scrum accidentally transferred from land to sea. The *Jessica* was a decent-sized boat but Bob's wheelchair took up much of the space and even without that, it was comically cramped and I was surprised to see that Bouncer was there.

Tim saw my look and said, 'I've made Bouncer an honorary member of the network. We've had a chat and he understands the ground rules.'

I was about to open the briefing but Kate said, 'if you don't mind John, I'd like to say something.'

I moved aside to let her take the central position, which left her jammed between me and Marie.

'I hope you all enjoyed the anatomy refresher course,' she began, with a small smile in Marie's direction.

There was some laughter, but it was carefully subdued. No-one was sure yet how she was going to continue.

'We've heard a lot of nonsense talked this morning,' she continued, 'and it's time for some serious straight talking. I knew John was going to the wedding. I knew he'd be sharing a room with Marie. Nothing that went on there has affected my relationship with him.'

It sounded as though she had chosen the phrase carefully, and it still wasn't very reassuring, even when she reached out and touched my hand.

'I've persuaded Marie to stay on,' Kate said. 'The *Jurassic Star* is my boat and I figure the best way to kill off any idea there is some kind of tug-of-love going on is to invite her to stay on board and, for the record, I am not pregnant and I'm not planning to marry John.'

There wasn't much warmth in the statement but the atmosphere in the saloon did relax a little. It was clear everyone was relieved there was not going to be an overtly poisonous situation on board the boat, on top of what was happening outside.

Then Kate turned to what she clearly regarded as the main issue.

'In any event,' she said, 'it's not certain I'll be here much longer. There's a good chance Ocean Reports will want me out.'

Cutting off the expressions of sympathy, Kate spelled out the details.

'I haven't been formally fired,' she said, 'I've just been shunted aside. Someone else is being sent to in to take control of the coverage and I'm to be allowed to help as far my situation allows.'

'I hate to say this, Kate,' Chunk said, 'but they have got a point. We are more or less under lockdown here. I've been out to check and there must be a hundred hacks within spitting distance.'

Kate did not look impressed. Usually Chunk was a master of tact, but the remark only added to the prickly atmosphere. Sensing that things could easily go seriously pear-shaped, Birdy suggested that we take a break to get some drinks organised as there didn't seem to be any chance of getting out to a pub. The scrum untangled itself again and Tim and Lottery got some beers from the galley.

When we had all settled down again, I asked Jay, who was cramped in one corner, hunched over his laptop, to give us an update on what was running on the Internet.

'Before I do,' he said, 'I'd just like to say I've been taking a very close look at the photo of Marie.'

There were few smiles but it was clear he was completely serious.

'I'm virtually certain it was taken from a drone,' he said. 'As most of you know, I've been working with photographic drones for the past year and I'd say, without much doubt, that photo was a still out of video footage taken by an aerial drone.'

I saw my chance and jumped in. 'If it was part of a video, at least there won't be any more shocks to come. Nothing happened. Marie was just teasing me a bit,' I said, eager to re-enforce the point.

I saw Marie was hesitating, wondering whether to say something, so I added quickly, 'and it makes sense that it was a drone. That room isn't overlooked from anywhere else in the Auberge.'

'This is not good,' Tim said, 'first off, they managed to find out John was going to France, which wasn't widely known. And if they thought it was worthwhile to send somebody with a drone after him, that means they are not kidding.'

'No doubt about that anyway,' I said, 'that press conference was very carefully orchestrated. Even if they hadn't spotted Marie at the end, it would still have been a complete rout. The full story was planned and scheduled to run on UpstairsBackstairs whether Marie had come to Weymouth or not.'

Jay went on with his report and nothing much had changed. UpstairsBackstairs was still setting the news and social media agenda. The respectable parts of the media were adding the usual 'unconfirmed reports' and 'firm denials' but the basic narrative was unchanged. Everyone was asking the same questions: were Kate and I planning to get married? Was Kate pregnant? Had Marie arrived in Weymouth to try to win me back? Was Kate going to lose her sailing sponsorship because of a sordid love triangle?

We had just started discussing what kind of denials would be of any use, when Inspector Frampton arrived.

'Looks like you need a bit more space to do your drinking,' he said, looking around the cabin. I've been trying to see what we can do about that.

'I'm sure Chief Inspector Hunter will back me up,' he began, nodding towards Rachel, 'when I say I'm under considerable pressure to handle this situation delicately. The marina is completely surrounded by the media.

'There's no shortage of police in Weymouth, in fact they've drafted in enough to fill one of the local holiday camps, but so far, I'm not being allowed to divert any of them from Games security. That may change but for the moment, I have to manage with my local men.

'So,' Frampton continued, 'I've called in a few favours. The marina manager is an old friend of mine and he doesn't want any more trouble than he's got already with this pack of hysterical hacks swarming around his domain. Between us we've rounded up some equipment to get you ashore safely. There's a circus over in Dorchester and they've agreed to lend us a tented tunnel which we can rig between your boat and the car park. In the car park itself we will rig a tent at the end of the tunnel big enough to hold vehicles.'

'They'll know all our cars already,' I said.

'Indeed they will,' Frampton said, 'so I've arranged to get you another vehicle. One of the local hire companies is run by another friend of mine. He's got a nine-seat people carrier with tinted windows which he uses mainly for hen nights. He will give you a very good rate on that if you wouldn't mind hiring it. The tent won't cost you anything. The marina is willing to foot that bill.'

'Do you want us to put balloons and pink ribbons on it,' Tim asked.

Frampton smiled. 'That won't be necessary.'

'It all sounds fine,' I said, 'and we're very grateful but where are we going to go in this hen night limo?'

'That's the tough one,' Frampton said. 'I don't see how you'll be able to watch the sailing. The last thing I need is a fight with the hacks in the middle of the crowd watching on the big screens on the beach or at the cliff-top. Our best hope is that this shambles will lose its momentum but, in the meantime, I'm sure we can find you some quiet places to drink and watch on TV. You should be able to get out of Weymouth if you need to. I know this is a bastard but I need your cooperation.'

At that point, Frampton's cell phone rang. He apologised and took the call.

'There's a woman called Sandra Snow here to see you. She says she's been sent by Ocean Reports.'

'That will be my replacement,' Kate said icily, 'we'd better let her in.'

'Are you being replaced?' Frampton asked.

'Not completely, just pushed aside for now.'

'I'm very sorry to hear that,' Frampton said and he sounded as though he meant it. 'We'll try and get this mess under control as quickly as we can.'

Birdy went out onto the quay and escorted Sandra Snow into the cabin. She was a dark-haired, tall young woman who looked as though she was barely into her 20s. She was wearing the sailors' unofficial uniform of sweatshirt and loose-fitting tracksuit bottoms and she was clearly nervous.

We all waited while Birdy made the introductions then Sandra turned to Kate. 'I'm really sorry about all this,' she said. 'I've always admired your exploits and I'm a genuine fan. I know this is embarrassing for both of us but I hope we can get along.'

'I'm sure we will,' Kate said coolly. 'Why don't you tell us something about yourself?'

What followed was a fascinating contest between the two women. There was clearly a battle going on, but the two women were struggling with themselves not with each other. Kate was struggling to be calm and professional, while I knew that her natural instinct was to send Sandra flying into the harbour. Sandra was clearly in awe of Kate and the rest of the people in the cabin, but at the same time she was determined to project an image of confidence and by and large she did it very well.

'I work for a sailing magazine, based in Poole down the coast,' Sandra said, 'but I used to work for the *Dorset Echo* here in Weymouth, so I'm very familiar with the sailing scene. I sail myself,' she turned towards Kate, 'but I'm 1000 miles from your league. However, I know most of the competitors because I reported on their visits for the preliminary trials, while they were getting used to the water, though I know the Americans a lot less well than you do.'

She turned back to the group. 'Let me just say one thing,' she said, 'I watched the press conference and I thought it was a total disgrace. It made me ashamed to be a journalist. You have my word that while I'm here I won't repeat anything I see or hear while I'm with you to anyone, journalist or not.'

Kate smiled. It wasn't very warm but at least it was a smile of sorts.

'That's good to hear,' she said, 'welcome aboard. It looks as though we have yet another honorary member of the Saxon Network, but I hope you've got somewhere to sleep.'

9

Then it was Birdy's turn to come under attack. We started the next day relatively peacefully. Kate and Sandra held a joint briefing and divided up the day's tasks. The meeting wasn't exactly cheerful but both women kept it amicable and no blood was shed. It was agreed that Sandra would do the main racing coverage and Kate would stay with the American team, operating mainly from their private complex, which was well shielded from the press. Kate also had Bouncer for extra protection.

The crowd of hacks besieging the marina had thinned down considerably but there was still enough to make it necessary for everyone to use the tunnel to get away smoothly. Rachel and Marie went to London, setting off early and travelling together by train. Marie wanted to make peace with her new British associates and Rachel was attending an inquest with her team into why her big case had collapsed.

Birdy and I were enjoying a quiet morning coffee in the cockpit of the *Jessica* when the news came almost simultaneously from Frampton and from Jay. Frampton called first. He had received a report from a policeman on patrol in the village of Fortuneswell, on Portland, that Birdy's helicopter had been vandalised at the farm where it was parked up for the duration of the Games. Almost immediately afterwards, Jay came with the news that the story had broken on UpstairsBackstairs.

The headline read: **Lieutenant-Commander 'Birdy' Sarum – the pilot who never grew up.** The story said that, once again, Birdy had been engaged in some daredevil low flying near Portland Bill to impress a woman, and had badly damaged the helicopter that had been loaned to him by Starling Aviation. The article went on to recount how Birdy had come by his nickname, how, in his early days in the Navy, he had clipped a tree top while flying low to impress a girlfriend and then told the CO it was a bird strike – while admitting that the bird was in its nest at the time. The story said the original exploit had been considered a daring bit of fun by a young lieutenant, but Starling Aviation, unlike the CO at the time, did not see the joke and was planning to sue Birdy for the damage.

Rubbing salt still further into the wound, the article described Birdy's distinguished naval background. It listed the seven admirals in his family and contrasted their distinguished service from Napoleonic times to the

Falklands with Birdy's madcap, frivolous approach to his career. The article ended with the comment that it was unlikely that Birdy was going to be able to persuade any aviation company to lend him helicopters in the future, as they were doing now.

Birdy did a good job of keeping his composure but I could see he was badly shaken by the article. Frampton wanted us to come straight away to Portland and everyone else came along to get away from the boat for a while. Lottery was torn between trying to make up with his girlfriend, who had gone off shopping in Weymouth in a huff at being neglected, and getting in on any action there might be in Portland. In the end the possibility of action won.

We drove up in Tim's car, with Jay following in his Range Rover, which was packed with his technical equipment. When we reached the farm, I fully expected to find journalists there but there was only Frampton and an elderly constable called Vic, who was obviously a Portlander. While Frampton made the introductions, Jay checked the Internet and confirmed that neither the UpstairsBackstairs story nor the growing number of social media posts gave any location more specific than Portland. When we inspected the damage to the Bell Jet Ranger we saw why. The damage to the under section was severe, but close examination showed it could only have been caused by vandalism, not by careless flying. In contrast, the images on UpstairsBackstairs had been digitally doctored to make the accident story look much more plausible. It was obviously a deliberate decision by Maxine Herald to keep the press away. If any of the hacks did happen to have any flying experience, they would have spotted immediately that the damage was a set-up. We showed the Internet stories to Frampton who grasped straightaway what was going on.

'They really have it in for you, don't they,' he said, then asked Vic to repeat his report for us. The constable said a farmworker had seen two men leave the field where the helicopter was parked and get into a grey Ford Focus. He said the car had driven off in the direction of Portland Bill, not towards Weymouth.

'That's a help,' Frampton said, 'but I don't have the manpower to organise a full-blown search.' He turned to me, 'looks like the same vehicle that was involved in the attempt to snatch Kate at the quayside.'

'You weren't fooled then.'

'Hardly!'

'We'll carry out the search ourselves,' I said.

'Let me take care of that,' Jay said.

Frampton glanced at Jay's artificial foot and hesitated, obviously concerned not to offend. Jay smiled. 'Don't worry, Inspector, I'm not planning to trek across Portland. I have a drone that will do the job.'

Frampton looked intrigued. 'I'm not sure that's legal, but I'm not going to ask,' he said, 'but we need a chat first.'

While Jay set up his equipment, Frampton gathered the rest of us in a small group out of earshot of the constable.

'If you find the men who did this,' he said, 'you hand them over to me.'

'We'll need to talk to them first,' Birdy said.

Frampton hesitated for a moment then said quietly, 'on one condition.'

'Which is?'

'I hope you've gathered by now that I'm on your side,' he said, 'I knew you'd recognised the man who grabbed Kate at the marina and I've tried as best I can to protect you from the press but understand this: all cooperation between us ends if you hurt these men when you catch them. Talk to them by all means, but I don't want any SAS-style interrogations or even psychological intimidation. I want them handed over to me physically and mentally as you found them. Is that quite clear?'

'I was about to give Frampton a reluctant promise, but Tim beat me to it.

'If it is Kit Sanders he'll tell us what's going on. I guarantee it,' Tim said. 'He was in Afghanistan as a contractor while I was there. I know him well. There won't be any need for violence I promise.'

'Fair enough,' Frampton said, looking relieved, 'let's have a look at this wonderful toy you've got.'

While we had been talking, Jay had been busy. From an aluminium case in the back of the Range Rover he had unpacked a drone with a video camera slung below its central crosspiece. In the back seat, he had set up a reinforced military laptop with a large separate battery attachment. We all watched, fascinated, as he brought onto the screen a software program which contained diagrams of every standard British car, van and truck.

'You said it was a Ford Focus?'

Frampton nodded.

Jay spun quickly through the vehicle images on the screen until he found the Ford page. 'Is that the right model?' he asked, indicating the largest of the Focus models.

'I don't want my local man to see all this,' Frampton said, 'but I'm pretty sure that's the model he meant.'

Jay explained that the camera on the drone was now programmed to look for that shape of vehicle and once identified, it would flash back a warning to the control centre.

'I'm going to allow this,' Frampton said, 'but for God's sake be careful. As far as I know there are no small aircraft on Portland at the moment. Just make sure you don't hit the lighthouse or any of the other buildings.'

Jay laughed. 'Don't worry, Inspector, I've spent a whole year flying these things. I know what I'm doing.'

Unsurprisingly, there were no immediate results. We all sat crouched in the back of the Range Rover, watching as the drone circled over the open fields and abandoned quarries which were the main features of the Portland landscape. Each time Jay spotted any habitation or cluster of vehicles he guided the drone in and hovered over the area. In most cases, the program wasn't needed to identify any vehicles as the shapes were visible enough thanks to the high definition lens of the camera. The program came into its own only once, when the drone hovered over a small car park where a number of cars and vans were partially covered by the canopies of surrounding trees. Despite the foliage, the drone could identify vehicle shapes but there was no Ford Focus.

After half an hour, Jay brought the drone back to change the battery then sent it off towards the village of Easton where there was more traffic. Once again, we had no immediate luck. Then suddenly the laptop sounded the warning beep and we saw it had locked onto a grey Ford Focus pulling away from a small cottage, not far from the village square.

'It has to be them,' Frampton said, 'looks as though they're heading towards the lighthouse.'

They're not going there as tourists,' I said, 'they're more likely looking for somewhere to eat. It is nearly lunchtime.'

We set off in convoy. I drove the Range Rover with Birdy beside me and Frampton crouching beside Jay as he controlled the drone in the back. Tim and Lottery followed behind. I drove slowly with Jay giving me directions, accompanied by a running commentary from Frampton.

They were heading towards the lighthouse.

'If they are going to eat,' Frampton said, 'there are really only two likely places. There's the Lobster Pot near the lighthouse and the Pulpit which is a bit further away.'

'Are they the kind of places we could get them out of easily?' I asked.

'Be easier if they chose the Pulpit,' Frampton said. 'It's divided into several rooms and there is enough space to move around. They both get pretty crowded at lunchtime but the Lobster Pot only has one big room and the tables are very close together. If they sit outside, it would be easier but those tables get taken early on in the good weather.'

'Where will they park?'

'If they go to the Lobster Pot, they'll have to park in the main Bill car park. The Pulpit has a parking area of its own.'

We stayed well behind the Ford Focus, as the drone was delivering a very clear picture of where they were heading, and in the end they did choose the Pulpit. We gave them time to park and go inside and then pulled up out of sight to give Jay the chance to bring down the drone inconspicuously. We attracted the curiosity only of a couple of birdwatchers who looked annoyed that we might be disturbing the wildlife. But they made no comment and walked on, leaving Jay to retrieve the drone and pack it away. We held a quick council of war and I could see that Frampton was nervous about whether we were going to keep our word. We agreed that we would go into the Pulpit and get them out, and I promised Frampton once again that we would be absolutely discreet and there would be no disturbance or violence whatever.

'Best me and Lottery do the talking,' Tim said, 'you and Birdy stay out of the way and block the exit just in case they make a run for it.'

Lottery grinned at Frampton. 'Don't worry Inspector, that's not going to happen.'

'When we get inside,' Tim said, 'we'll join them at their table. When you come in, keep well away but let them see that you are there.'

The entrance to the Pulpit was at the top of a short flight of stone steps. Inside, there was a narrow corridor leading to the bar. There, the corridor divided, leading into two separate dining areas, one at ground level, the other accessed by a few wooden steps. Tim and Lottery went in first and we followed a few moments later. By the time we were inside, they had already located Sanders and Waugh and joined them at a table in the upper dining area.

I don't think any of the diners could have known anything odd was going on. As soon as he sat down, Tim started chatting in a very friendly way, as though he was greeting old friends. Lottery called over the waitress and ordered some coffee. I could see Frampton was reassured but he had only a side view of Sanders's face. From where I was sitting, I could see his eyes and read the fear in them. They talked for about ten minutes. There were moments when the conversation seemed intense but it always looked friendly. I could see that Frampton was watching Tim and Lottery for any signs of movement under the table, but both men kept their hands clearly in sight and their feet well away from Sanders and Waugh. After a further five minutes, all four got up and made for the door. Tim signalled us to come over.

'This is Inspector Frampton of the Weymouth police,' Tim said, 'you know Birdy and John of course.'

They both shook hands with Frampton and nodded towards us. To a casual passer-by, it was a normal social introduction but I could see Sanders was terrified. Waugh looked sullen and resigned rather than afraid and had probably decided to go along with whatever Sanders agreed to.

'Kit and Mike have agreed to cooperate with us,' Tim said, 'we're going back to the cottage they've rented in Easton. They have something to show us and they'd like you to come along.'

The formality of it was almost laughable. There was nothing 'Kit and Mike' wanted less than to have to go anywhere with us, but there was clearly going to be no resistance.

Outside, Tim and Lottery got into their car with Sanders and Waugh and we followed.

The cottage was very close to where the drone had originally spotted the Ford Focus. It was a small, neglected terraced house in a narrow side street off the square. We all found parking spaces and went inside.

Without speaking, Sanders went into the bedroom and came back with a laptop. He fired it up and we watched as he brought his email inbox onto the screen. He scrolled down and opened an email from Red Associates.

'Who are Red Associates?' Birdy asked.

'Kit doesn't know,' Tim said, 'they received a phone call from one of Ray Vossler's men to await instructions by email and this came.'

The email was lengthy and detailed. It described Birdy's helicopter and gave the postcode and map coordinates of where it was parked. It went on to instruct that the machine was to be damaged and said details were in the attachment. The deadline for the work to be completed was 0900 that morning. Sanders clicked on the attachment, which contained a detailed diagram showing exactly where the damage was to be caused. Below it, was a list of suggestions of what tools to use and how best to do the job.

'You're not going to be able to find who the sender was easily,' Kit said. 'Everyone who works with them knows there's no point in trying.'

Tim turn to Frampton. 'Kit is happy to come to the station with you and make a full statement. I'm sure you wouldn't mind giving the details to Birdy, so that he can contact Starling Aviation.'

'What's going to happen to us?' Waugh asked.

'You'll be charged with committing criminal damage,' Frampton said, 'we'll get an assessor in. His report will determine which court you will appear in.'

'What about the email?' Waugh said.

'I wouldn't go there if I were you,' Frampton said, 'criminal damage is a matter of money. Conspiracy to commit criminal damage or conspiracy to defame Birdy here means prison time. We'll see you down at the station.'

He turned to me. 'What about the business of the marina with Kate?'

'We've discussed that,' Tim said, 'the decision must be yours of course, Inspector, but I'm sure Kate will not want to press charges. In fact I'm not even sure she will recognise Kit.'

'No emails about that?'

'Apparently not,' Tim said, 'that was just a phone instruction.'

Frampton grunted. 'If you say so. Let's get back to Weymouth. I have things to do.'

Taking Vic with him, Frampton put the two men in the back of his police car and they left the island and drove off back to Weymouth. I called Jay, who had been waiting out of sight in his Range Rover on the other side of the village. I waited until we were all together then said to Tim, 'what the hell did you say to them? They were like lambs.'

Tim laughed. 'We just talked about old times.'

'You've never had any old times with that arsehole.'

'Well, not exactly old times, more shared experiences. I asked Kit if he remembered what the Taliban used to do to a prisoner's hands when they were being interrogated. You remember. They used to cut the tendons starting between the thumb and the first finger. It made the hand into a kind of flipper.'

'You threatened them with that?' I said.

This time it was Lottery who laughed. 'There was no need to threaten,' he said, 'Sanders and Waugh are no heroes. We just asked them, in a conversational kind of way, if that were ever to happen to them, which hand did they think would be worst?'

'What did he say about Kate?' I asked.

'I'm afraid that's the bad news,' Tim said, 'it wasn't Vossler who ordered the attack.'

'Who then?'

'Ali Omar. They got a phone call saying Omar wanted Kate snatched and held somewhere. According to Sanders, Omar has it in you for personally. Seems he is in deep shit with his boss. Vossler blames him for letting them all get caught after the attack. Apart from anything else, Omar is scared shitless Vossler will fire him and leave him to pay his own legal fees. He blames you for that and is planning revenge. God knows what he would have done to Kate if they had got hold of her.'

10

When we got back to the *Jessica*, Chunk had arrived and with him was a tiny, academic-looking young woman, with short-cropped hair and a pair of unfashionable, heavy-rimmed glasses which gave her a distinctly owlish look. I recognised her face from her website photograph before Chunk introduced her as Sheila Cayman of the *New York Times*. We shook hands and I tried to examine her without staring, as I was sure I knew her from somewhere. When I had Googled her after Virginia Walsh had warned me she was coming, her professional life seemed to be centred entirely around Washington and New York. She had won a Pulitzer prize for an investigation into the pharmaceutical industry and another major award for one into the US securities markets, and I couldn't think where our paths could have crossed.

'Ms Cayman watched the press conference online and she has a very good grasp of the situation,' Chunk said.

That was Chunk code. It meant Cayman was someone to be reckoned with and I should be careful.

I introduced Birdy and after a few pleasantries, he suggested I take Cayman over to the *Jurassic Star*. 'Kate's not back yet,' he said, 'you shouldn't be disturbed.'

I led Cayman across the narrow gang-plank to the *Jurassic Star* which was deserted and quiet, except for the background noise of a television in the main saloon which was relaying one of the sailing events. It seemed almost like communication from another world. Though we were at the very centre of the sailing Olympics, the races seemed to be taking place in a parallel universe. I switched off the set and offered Cayman some coffee. She declined and we sat facing each other across the small chart table.

'You must have an amazing memory for faces,' she said, 'I could tell you recognised me.'

'I have looked at your website,' I said.

'But there's something else, isn't there? It's not just the website.'

'You're very quick,' I said. 'Yes, I do believe we've met, but I can't for the life of me remember where.'

'That's pretty impressive all the same,' she said. 'We haven't actually met. We've seen each other once.'

'Where?'

'The Reuters office in Amman. You walked through the newsroom with Sam Roberts on the way to his office. He didn't introduce me because I was on the phone and by the time you came out, I'd gone.'

Sam Roberts had been the Reuters bureau chief in Amman when I had lived there working for MI6. We had been good friends, and his wife had become very close to my wife, Sarah.

'You worked for Reuters? There was no mention on your website.'

'I never put it on my CV because I stayed with them less than six months. I knew straight away that agency life wasn't for me. I'm best when I'm concentrating on one story. But I was lucky. For my first posting I was number three in the Amman bureau. Sam was my mentor. When I said I needed to change direction, he was very sympathetic. It was Sam who introduced me to someone on the *Times*.

'You were the whizzkitten!'

Cayman laughed. 'Yes I know that was what Sam called me. It's not a nickname I've tried to keep up.'

I laughed too. 'Doesn't quite go with Pulitzer prizes, but Sam meant it as a real compliment. Sam thought the world of you. He said he thought you'd be general manager of Reuters while he was still pounding a keyboard.'

'Sam was very good to me and for me.'

'Did he say much about me?'

'Not really, but he did tell me about your wife's cooking. He said that when he arrived, you were listed in the bureau handover book as the best source in Amman, and there was a note to try to get invited to your house because your wife was such a fantastic cook.'

'Yes, I've heard that,' I said, 'it's true, her cooking was amazing.'

Without asking permission, Cayman took out her iPhone, and switched on the voice recorder. At the same time, she took out a notebook and pen.

'I gather you don't like talking about Sarah,' Cayman said.

'I don't want her brought into this.'

'I'm afraid it's too late for that.'

The switch in tone was barely perceptible but it was definitely there. She was still smiling and friendly, but she had just given me a flash of the woman who won awards for investigative journalism. She had been softening me up.

Her tone was just right, reassuring but indicating that she was there for a purpose. She had obviously got a lot of experience in interrogating without appearing to – but then so had I.

But we had started on the worst possible subject. Her remark about Sarah's cooking had taken me instantly back to Amman and the fun we had had together as she tried to teach me to cook. It was one of the few happy memories I had and it led on instantly to the many bitterly unhappy ones.

I tried to change the subject or at least stall while I cleared my head of the images.

'Before we start,' I said, 'tell me a bit about your briefing in Washington. Who did you talk to?'

Cayman didn't show any reluctance to answer the question.

'I had about twenty minutes with Mark Vossler, but we just chatted, then he handed me over to the deputy head of the Vossler group PR department, Marilyn Jacobson.'

'Why did they say they had contacted you?'

Again, Cayman answered smoothly.

'They said the story was about to break that you were intending to sue MI6 and it was important for me to know the background.'

'What did they say about Ray Vossler's role in the London terrorist attack?'

'Almost nothing. They said he was innocent, of course, but they didn't want to say anything that would jeopardise his defence if it ever came to trial.'

'If?'

'Yes that was the word they used. Now, let's get back to Sarah. Would you say your marriage was happy?'

I could see she wasn't going to be put off, so I decided to see how little I could get away with.

'At first very happy,' I said.

'And in Amman?'

'Well no, she wasn't happy there. Did Sam Roberts tell you what I was doing in Amman?'

'No, but the word around town was that you were a shady arms dealer and military fixer.'

'That about sums up my cover. I was an MI6 field officer and in a place like Amman it doesn't take long for people to figure out who the spooks are, so we had an 'official' agent.

'You mean Abel Rolph.'

I smiled. 'Yes, it wasn't a very well-kept secret, but that was deliberate. Having Abe there helped quite a bit. We were both there to gather intelligence, but my dodgy arms dealing was a very effective way of getting close to the serious players in the world of terrorism. I cut a pretty disreputable figure. That was also deliberate. It was also why Sarah became unhappy. She detested the people I had to socialise with.'

'People like Susan al-Maliki?'

'Why do you mention her? Sarah had nothing especially against Susan. She was my bridge partner. What has this got to do with anything?'

Cayman ignored my question.

'Your wife didn't play bridge?'

'She did, but she hated the country club. I had to go there to network with exactly the kind of people Sarah detested.'

'Did you sleep with al-Maliki?'

I don't think it was even meant to be a trick question. It was simply the next question on her list.

'No.'

'Never?'

'No. Susan was a British woman who had made an extremely unhappy marriage to a wealthy Jordanian businessman. She practically lived at the country club and she played bridge extremely well, even better than my wife incidentally.'

I stopped short.

'Before we go any further,' I said, 'I want to know what all this is about.'

'The Vosslers gave me al-Maliki's name. I couldn't speak to him personally but I Skyped with his PA. She said you were cited in al-Maliki's divorce.'

'That's absolute rubbish,' I said, 'complete and utter rubbish.'

'You didn't sleep around?'

'No!'

'Not even in Iraq. You were away from home a lot.'

'No,' I said, 'not even in Iraq.'

'OK. Tell me about the nude swimming parties?'

'The what? Who the hell have you been talking to?'

'A woman called Heather Fenton. The Vosslers gave me her name.'

'Oh for God's sake,' I said, 'Heather Fenton is one the most notorious gossips in the Middle East. She was the wife of the press secretary at the British Embassy – they're divorced now – but she was a total cow. She specialised in telling stories about everyone, especially the wives of colleagues. They were always wildly exaggerated and often just plain made up.'

'So you didn't hold nude swimming parties.'

I knew I had to be careful. We were long past the stage where I could simply dismiss Heather Fenton's stories as the ravings of a vicious social bitch. I was also having trouble thinking objectively about our social life at the time. I had always hated the house. I had originally found a wonderful Arab-style house, very similar to the one I had grown up in until my parents had been killed in a car crash. But it had been entirely unsuitable for my cover, and I had ended up in a luxurious but soul-less villa in the fashionable west side of the city.

'We only held one nude swimming party in the entire time I was in Amman,' I said, 'except it wasn't a party as such, and there were no strangers or outsiders. Everyone there was a close friend and most of them military. If you wander across to the *Jessica* later, you can ask Tim or Birdy about it. They were both there. Far from being an orgy, it was probably the only gathering in that house that I ever actually enjoyed. We were among friends, real friends – and we ate and drank until the early hours, and swam to sober up so we could drink some more.'

Cayman didn't comment but went on making notes as matter-of factly as if we had been discussing sailing prospects.

'When did Sarah first meet Ali Omar?' she said when she had finished writing.

'You know about the Arms Fair I attended in Rome, while I was investigating the corruption Vossler was involved in?' I began.

'I know about the Arms Fair, yes.'

There was something odd about the way she said it, but I couldn't be sure what.

'But your wife and Omar,' Cayman prompted.

'There was a party at a very chic Roman restaurant called the Ostaria del Orso to welcome delegates to the Fair. Omar sat next to Sarah. He started groping her. Not just a pat on the knee. He practically tried to strip her naked under her skirt. He is a total pig when it comes to women. I gave him a very serious warning but I tried to avoid a scene in the restaurant. Omar started a fight there and then, and we almost wrecked the place.'

'There is another, quite different view of all this.'

'Go on.'

'The Vosslers maintain that you set up shop in Amman but you actually enjoyed your undercover life. They say you turned your home into,' Cayman glanced down at her notes, 'a centre for dissolute and disreputable behaviour.' Heather Fenton confirms this. She says you held nude swimming parties which turned into orgies. She says you slept around both in Amman and while you were away on trips, and that drove Sarah to do the same.'

Cayman looked at me steadily, as if willing me to interrupt, but I steeled myself to let her finish.

'Vossler's people say you and Sarah were going through a particularly rocky patch and she said she wanted to go to Rome. You had no real business going there, so you invented a new angle to the corruption investigation. MI6 said there was nothing to investigate. In fact they told you specifically not to go the Arms Fair.

Cayman reached into her small note case and produced a piece of paper.

I recognised it immediately. The cable was from Vauxhall Cross, MI6 headquarters in London, specifically from Virginia Walsh, who had been overseeing my anti-corruption investigations. It had been decrypted and there were various blacked-out notations above and below the text that were not in MI6 standard format.

The message, however, was clear: it was a direct order not to proceed to the arms fair in Rome, as there were no grounds to continue my investigation there.

'I presume the Vossler got this from the CIA,' I said.

'Probably,' Cayman said. 'Did you receive it?'

'Yes.'

'And you ignored it?'

'Yes.'

'Why?'

'For a very good reason. My investigation into corruption in Iraq had led me right to Ray Vossler and I knew that most of his contacts would be at the Arms Fair. It was vital for me to go.'

'Why do you suppose you were warned off?'

'My masters didn't want to upset Washington. They thought American corruption was not our business, even though a lot of prominent Brits had become involved in Vossler's money-making schemes.'

'But you went anyway?'

'Yes, I did.'

'And you took your wife, Sarah, with you?'

'Yes.'

'Did you often take her on trips?'

'No, it was the first time.'

'The Vosslers say it was Sarah who talked you into going to Rome so she could continue her affair with Omar. They say Sarah thought the restaurant fight was exciting, and she started up again with Omar at the party at the Italian general's house to torment you. But things got complicated because another of Sarah's lovers turned up as well.'

'The Italian lieutenant?'

'Yes.'

'And when is she supposed to have had an affair with this lieutenant?'

'On the first day in Rome. You went off on your own, leaving Sarah to her own devices. She couldn't find Omar so she had a quick fling with the lieutenant.'

'And what is supposed to have happened at the party?'

'Omar was with Sarah. He found out about the lieutenant and had a row with her. She ran away. He followed her in the jeep, but she was so distraught she ran under the wheels and when the lieutenant tried to intervene, you hit him with a throat punch used by Special Forces and he died instantly.'

'Now it's my turn to ask a question?' I said, 'do you actually believe any of this shit.'

Cayman put down her pen and switched off the iPhone recorder and for the first time she appeared to relax.

'No, of course not', she said, with a broad smile.

Her response and her smile took me by surprise.

'You really don't.'

'No, it's all fabricated, of course.'

'You sounded as though you did believe at least some of it.'

Cayman laughed. 'I just wanted to see your reaction. But that doesn't mean the problem is solved.'

'What do you mean?'

'Here's the situation,' Cayman said. 'I do believe your version of events. I have been around Washington long enough to know what a crook Ray Vossler is. I've spoken to Sam – he's in Shanghai – and he sends his regards, by the way. He's told me exactly what kind of a silly bitch Heather Fenton is. Sam also told me about Sarah, and he says the idea she could have an affair with a pig like Omar beggars belief.'

'I'm very glad to hear it,' I said, 'but what I don't understand is why the Vosslers got you involved. They must know your reputation. They must know you wouldn't fall for all this.'

'Don't underestimate the Vosslers. They know how to play these games. They know I won't believe you, but they also know you can't actually disprove any of these allegations. They want the allegations in the *Times* as well as on the Internet. I can fill my article with your denials but the allegations will still be there.'

'But you'll say you believe me.'

'Yes I will, but they're counting on the constraints of the good old *New York Times* style, and I'm sure they know I've been in Amman. If I go too strongly in your favour without producing proof, they'll say they didn't realise I was an old friend. I told you, they are experts when it comes to games like these.'

'I have no proof to give you.'

'Not even on the corruption.'

'No. After my arrest in Rome, they confiscated my laptop and every document they could find. There was backup material in Amman but someone broke into my house and got that too.'

'What about MI6?'

'They have copies of everything I reported before I left Amman. But they're not about to give it to me. Virginia Walsh says it's too inconclusive to be of any use. They still don't want to start a feud with the United States.'

'The sex stuff is easy to make stick,' Cayman said. 'Even though Heather Fenton is the mother of all bitches, she can be very convincing.'

'We agree this has nothing to do with my suing MI6?'

'Of course. This is a campaign to discredit you before Vossler goes to trial, if he ever does. My bet is that you are going to be facing a torrent of abuse on UpstairsBackstairs that, if you're not careful, is going to overwhelm you. I'm afraid you and your network are all seriously out of your depth.

'This is not your kind of fight. It'll be like being caught in relentless crossfire without the weapons to fight back.'

It was at that cheerful point in the conversation that Birdy came sprinting over the gang plank and burst into the cabin.

'Jesus Christ, John,' he shouted. 'They're out. Out on bail. All of them. Ray Vossler is going to hold a press conference at 8 o'clock.'

11

It was a scramble to get ourselves organised in time for the press conference and nobody was in the mood to deal with it. We assembled in the main saloon of the *Jessica* and although we handled the space problem a bit better this time, the atmosphere was tense and fractious. Cayman had left immediately, saying she needed to do some more research, but would watch the press conference. I had a frustrating spell on the phone which turned out to be a complete waste of time. Sir Alastair was in court and couldn't be reached and Virginia would not take my calls.

Meanwhile, Kate was in a foul temper. She had given up trying to take part in the coverage of the Games altogether. She had, as she put it, spent the whole bloody afternoon hiding behind Bouncer while he fended off people trying to interview her, and she had left the coverage to Sandra. She had agreed with bad grace to come across to the *Jessica* but her mind was clearly not on the Vossler problem. Rachel and Marie were back from London and neither had achieved what they wanted. I gathered, through quick exchanges, that the inquest into the Finwell trial had not been resolved to anyone's satisfaction and Marie had not succeeded in persuading her future colleagues to set a start date for their collaboration.

Chunk also seemed quite distracted, which was uncharacteristic. He had a way of being able to focus very clearly on the problem in hand, despite his generally languid manner but, like Kate, his attention was not really on the Vosslers. Tim was trying to cheer Rachel up and Lottery was in a listless mood as his new girlfriend had given up on the whole thing and gone back to London. He was, however, making an effort to control it, though, as he took over looking after Cronin, when Leslie delivered him reluctantly to join the melee.

We managed to group ourselves so we could all see the television, which was tuned to the BBC News channel. At the same time Jay and Marie were both scanning the screens of their laptops. Jay was monitoring UpstairsBackstairs, while Marie checked on social networking.

I was surprised that the US Embassy had agreed to host this press conference but clearly the other Vossler brothers, Ivan and Mark, had enough credibility in Washington to force the issue. Ivan and Mark were known as the acceptable face of private equity, in contrast to Ray Vossler, who was always kept behind the scenes as much as possible. Ray's function was to launder large amounts of dodgy capital and funnel it into the Vossler Group, while staying out of the public eye. The older brothers had good war records and strong connections both on Capitol Hill and within the Intelligence community. With their weight behind Ray I knew anything might be about to happen.

When the press conference opened, it was clearly designed as a piece of theatre as much as a vehicle for conveying information. Ivan and Mark took centre stage, with Ivan controlling the microphone. They were flanked by the head of the Vossler group's legal team, Lewis Olsen and the deputy PR, Marilyn Jacobson. Ray Vossler was right at the end of the line, positioned so that any photos of him would have as background the Stars and Stripes and the Great Seal of the United States, which decorated the wall behind his section of the platform. There was no sign of Ali Omar or anyone else who had taken part in the attack.

Ivan began by thanking the ambassador for allowing the press conference to take place. The ambassador nodded in acknowledgement. He had the air of a man who was ill at ease, but who had a lifetime of experience in not showing it. Ivan went on to apologise to the press, saying that he was limited in what he could say as he was concerned not to interfere with the due process of the British legal system. I was quite sure Ivan would not let himself be limited by any such trivial consideration, and I was quickly proved right.

'We have come over to support our brother, Ray, who is in danger of suffering a grave injustice,' Ivan said. 'Over the past few weeks, you have been reading about the heroics of the so-called 'Saxon Network', who claim to have foiled a terrorist attack on London.'

Ivan paused for a full five seconds to emphasise the drama of what he was about to say, then, staring straight into the cameras he said, 'in reality, the Saxon Network are a bunch of grandstanding glory-seekers who managed to disrupt one of the most important American intelligence operations that has been undertaken in recent years.

'It has hitherto been classified as top secret, but I can now reveal that my brother and his associates were conducting a sting operation which would have exposed an Iranian terrorist cell capable of doing incalculable damage in Europe. Naturally, we hope and believe that this issue will never come to trial but, because of the ridiculous accusations made by John Saxon and his colleagues, we must be very cautious in what we say today. However, I can assure you that my brother will be able to prove beyond any doubt that he was acting on behalf of United States intelligence, as well as in the interests of our friends here in Britain.'

'Does that mean he was working for the CIA?' someone shouted from the back.

'All details of that kind will have to be reserved for the legal process,' Ivan said, then added, smiling, 'but I'm sure you can draw your own conclusions.'

There was a general clamour within the body of the press conference and almost a complete silence in the saloon of the *Jessica*. It was Cronin who spoke first.

'They'll never get away with this, they can't, they just can't.'

Before anyone else could comment, Jay said, 'it's started. You can see how they're going to play it. Ivan mouthing platitudes in London, while UpstairsBackstairs pours out the venom.'

The first headline set the tone. **The Saxon Network. Glory-seekers who ruined the chance to smash terrorist plot.**

What followed, I had to admit, was brilliantly done. A news stream was opened which recounted the whole story of the terrorist plot, but reversing and upending every detail.

There was an interview with Pete Zwiebeck, the germ warfare expert at USAMRIID, who had first been approached by the Vosslers. Now, however, he maintained that he had been approached by the Iranians and that Ray Vossler had persuaded him to provide bubonic plague germs to them despite his own misgivings, in order to take part in a sting operation. Zwiebeck admitted having been installed at the Vosslers' expense on a private island in the Bahamas, where he had held meetings with the Iranians.

In a curiously studied tone which suggested careful rehearsal, Zwiebeck stated that his meetings with Vossler had been to brief him on what the Iranians were up to, turning back to front the reality that Vossler had been coaching him on how entice the Iranians in. The same mirror reversal continued in the rest of his narrative of the preparation for the attack in London.

'We can prove this is total shit,' Cronin said angrily. 'We have tapes, we have details, we have everything to blow them out of the water.'

'But is Delgado up to it?' I said. 'Last time I saw him he was on the verge of a nervous breakdown, if not actually the middle of one.'

Vince Delgado was the ex-CIA operative who originally revealed the whole scheme to Cronin, but he had become terrified in the final stages of the operation.

When Cronin didn't answer, I said more calmly, 'where is Delgado now?'

Cronin didn't look me in the eye. 'He's in Australia, but we can get him back.'

I shook my head. 'You know there's no point. Delgado could never stand up against the Vosslers in court or anywhere else. We'll have to use his brother.'

The brother, Leo, was a former San Francisco police officer and altogether more rugged than Vince. He had replaced Vince in the final stage of our operation and knew more than enough to disprove this new Vossler version of events. Cronin looked relieved but before we could say any more, I switched my attention back to the television screen. While watching the UpstairsBackstairs travesty unfold on Marie's laptop, I had been keeping half an ear on the press conference as Ivan smiled and fenced politely with the press.

Then Ivan said suddenly, 'before I close, ladies and gentlemen, I'd like to say a few words about Kate Allison.

'As many of you may know, the Vossler Group is very involved in ocean racing and I have to say that I am a great admirer of Kate and all her notable achievements. I'm extremely sad to see such a fine woman being dragged down by John Saxon, who we all know as a failed Intelligence operative whose dissolute lifestyle caused the ruin and eventual death of his wife, and is now in the process of ruining the career of this fine yachtswoman, making her pregnant while two-timing her with a former lover at the same time. We only hope Kate can find some way of extricating herself from the clutches of a man disowned by his own intelligence service.'

I tried to make my way across the cabin to be with Kate but Jay interrupted.

'Looks like that was a cue,' he said, 'there's another news stream opening and it doesn't look good.'

The headline for the new stream was: **Five Reasons why the Saxon Network is disintegrating into chaos.**

Each section had a short paragraph followed by a link button to what it called 'evidence'.

I was named first.

John Saxon the failed spook with a Lawrence of Arabia complex, was the headline. This was over a photograph of me in the white Arab robe I had often worn while undercover in operations in Iraq and elsewhere in the Middle East.

John Saxon has been exposed as a failed spook who disobeyed his own intelligence service when they told him his work was getting nowhere. While based in Amman, Jordan, Saxon ran a notorious house of ill-repute, cheating on his wife and driving her into sluttish behaviour that eventually led to her death. Now love-rat John is wrecking the sailing career of Kate Allison. Kate is pregnant and Saxon is seeking consolation with his old mistress, who still believes in his phoney glamour. The link button led to the same cable Cayman had shown me, ordering me not to go to the Rome Arms Fair and there was a second link to a video interview with Heather Fenton.

The interview was another very clever piece of work. Fenton had obviously been coached by the Vossler legal team, as she managed to cram the maximum amount of innuendo into a short interview, without making any directly slanderous statements. But it was all there: the nude-swimming parties verging on orgies and my supposed adultery with Susan al-Maliki, which was illustrated with a damning photograph. In the photo, I had my arm round Susan, with a glass of champagne in the other hand and we were both smiling warmly at each other. The photo had been skilfully doctored to hide the fact that we were on a dais at the Amman Country Club, in front of a large audience, celebrating our winning the club's annual bridge tournament.

'If I'd known you had orgies, I'd have come to your house more often,' Tim said, but his attempt at a joke did nothing to lighten the mood and the news stream rolled relentlessly on.

Birdy was next. **Lieutenant Commander Birdy Sarum says goodbye to promotion as he continues his flying pranks.**

Birdy – the pilot who won't grow up - was hoping to make Commander this year, but there's no chance of that now as he goes on wrecking other peoples' helicopters with his daredevil fun and games.

Birdy's link went to a re-hash of the accusation that he had frivolously damaged the aircraft he currently had on loan, then came a headline that took everyone by surprise.

While Birdy's career flounders, Major 'Chunk' Kingsland-Manderby pursues his at everyone's expense.

Major Chunk's father is dying and his brother is ill. His estate is going to rack and ruin. The livelihoods of his tenants and workers are in jeopardy but does Chunk care? No. He's up for a big promotion. The rest can go to hell.

The link was simply to a photograph of the Kingsland-Manderby estate.

We all looked at Chunk but his face remained impassive.

'I'll tell you about it at the debrief,' he said and went back to looking over Jay's shoulder at the laptop screen.

I saw from the television that the press conference was over but the new stream certainly wasn't and it was Rachel who came under fire next.

Top cop neglects biggest case of her career for a bit of fun on the beach. The headline was over a photo of Rachel sunbathing topless, lying beside Tim.

What is it about the women who hang around the Saxon Network that makes them strip off all the time? the text began. This was followed by a close-up of Rachel's breasts, side by side with a similar one of Marie's, enlarged from the drone photo taken at the Auberge des Fleurs.

Chief Inspector Rachel would have done better to put her bra back on and concentrate on the Finwell case. Her colleagues are saying it's all gone tits up because she neglected the evidence gathering. Was it worth it Rachel? We don't think so.

'The cunning bastards,' Tim said, 'that photo was taken months ago, long before the Finwell trial,' then suddenly he jumped to his feet. 'Oh my God,' he shouted, 'what the hell is that?'

'Does the lovely Rachel know she's throwing away her career for a coward? Sergeant Major Tim Overton faces possible dismissal from the SAS.

The headline ran over a piece of text far more devastating than anything that had run before. The one word every soldier fears is cowardice and Tim watched ashen-faced as the accusation unfolded on the screen.

The United States Department of Defense has made a formal request to its British counterpart to investigate charges of cowardice in the face of the enemy on the part of Sgt Major Tim. The charges relate to a joint US-British operation in Afghanistan to rescue a young American female aid worker held hostage by the Taliban. The operation failed because Overton chickened out at the last moment and refused to lead the British team into action. The hostage was later killed by the Taliban.

The link was equally devastating. It was a video interview with the dead woman's father in which he said he had 'received information' that his daughter's death had been caused by Overton's refusal to commit to the action.

I looked at the faces around me, aghast. In all the years I had known them, I had never seen my 'network' of friends in such disarray. These were battle-hardened comrades in arms who had dealt countless times with every kind of danger, but this was totally different and we all knew it. It was as though we had all been caught in an ambush, like total greenhorns, without ammunition or body armour, with absolutely no idea how to respond to this massive barrage of 'incoming' malicious misinformation. We had gone from being out-manoeuvred to a total rout.

I stood up and called everyone sharply to order.

'We need a debrief,' I said. 'Right now.'

As I spoke, there was a clatter on the quayside gangway and Inspector Frampton and Bouncer arrived.

'The press are going mad out there,' Frampton said, 'I need to know what you plan to do.'

Kate pushed her way forward.

'Why don't we just sail out,' she said, 'no-one can think straight cooped up like this.'

'Great idea,' I said, but Tim shook his head. 'I have too many calls to make. I've got to find out what the hell is going on. I may have to go back to Hereford.' Rachel and Chunk also said they couldn't leave straightaway.

'Leaving is not that simple anyway,' Frampton said. 'The bridge to the outer harbour doesn't open again until eight-am tomorrow. Anyway, the press will follow you for sure, then there will be chaos.'

'Can we sail out tomorrow morning?' I said, 'or are you saying you want to smuggle us out of Weymouth altogether.'

I knew that was the solution Frampton wanted, but it was Bouncer who found the answer.

'Why don't they use my Dad's boat?' he said to Frampton, 'it's already in the outer harbour. They could set sail in the early hours tomorrow.'

'Do you mean in a fishing trawler?' Kate said.

Bouncer laughed. 'No, we have a yacht. It's a classic boat. Been in the family for ever. Believe me Kate, you'll love it.'

I looked around the still silent group.

'Sounds perfect,' I said, 'are we agreed? We stay on board tonight and debrief at sea tomorrow.'

12

That night, Bob Cronin had a heart attack. Fortunately, it happened when he was still on board the *Jurassic Star* and there were five people with him who were skilled in first-aid. We carefully adjusted his position, reassured him and the emergency services arrived before he needed CPR.

The paramedic told us he had been very lucky and he thought Bob would survive. Frampton managed to keep the press at bay and Leslie arrived soon after the ambulance. When I told Leslie what had happened he looked at me with the old mixture of anger and sorrow I knew so well from earlier times, his indulgence for his partner's desire to stay in the intelligence world gone in an instant. When we offered to go to the hospital with him, he was almost in tears as he pleaded with us not to.

'Please, John, please just leave him alone. He's not fit for this intelligence shit. He loves it but he's just not up to it. Please leave us alone once and for all, I beg you!'

I knew Leslie was right. The heart attack had been brought on by a phone call which had shaken all of us, but for Bob it had been just too much. We were discussing how to deal with the way the Vosslers had turned the terrorist attack on London into a supposed sting operation by simply taking the truth and turning it on its head. Only two of our people could turn it the right way up again and we had set about contacting them.

The first call was only a token one. Vince Delgado had tracked the relationship between Ray Vossler and the Iranians and would have been the ideal person, but during the operation his nerve had broken and he was now recuperating with his family in Australia. We had made a call to Melbourne but only to tell Vince what was going on and that we did not expect anything from him. We had been right. He had screamed 'I can't, I can't' before we even asked a question. Asking Vince to give evidence in any kind of court or to make any public statement where he would be challenged by the Vosslers was totally out of the question.

Next we tried his brother Leo, the retired San Francisco policeman who had taken over in the last stage of the operation. We had trouble tracking him down but didn't realise at first anything was wrong. It was late afternoon, San Francisco time, and we simply assumed Leo was out. We called his cell-phone two or three times then later we tried his home again and this time got his distraught wife. She said Leo was dead, killed by a hit-and-run driver two hours earlier. It was obvious to all of us that this was no accident and it was then that Bob had suffered his heart attack.

When the ambulance had left, I called everyone together and we agreed that we would carry on dealing with our individual problems as best we could, then get some sleep and rendezvous at 5:30 AM to be transferred, once again under guard, to Bouncer's boat.

My own first concern was to talk to my sons. I reached my sister-in-law in Canada, who was taking care of them, and I wasn't surprised to find the whole family knew everything that was going on. I spoke to each of my sons in turn and reassured them that everything they were seeing on the Internet was complete fabrication. I warned them that the Vosslers were engaged in a cleverly-designed campaign to distort the truth and they would hear more lies before we would be able to put things right. I emphasized that we'd clear it up, but that it would take time and they must remain strong in the meantime. I tried to keep the tone of the conversation as light as possible and they were old enough to share some jokes about my allegedly sexy lifestyle in Amman, but they weren't able to hide their concern. They asked about Kate and I assured them she wasn't pregnant and we had no plans to marry, but I added that I hoped they'd meet her soon, as I knew they would like her.

When I'd finished the call, Chunk called us together and apologised for not having confided in us earlier. He said it was true his father was gravely ill and was not expected to survive. He said it was also true that his elder brother had heart problems and had doubts about whether he would be fit enough to run the estate, if and when he did inherit. What was not true, Chunk said, was that he had committed himself to remaining in the army whatever happened. He said there were a couple of other options being considered and he promised to keep us posted in future. He spoke calmly, in a quiet conversational tone, but we could see that the Internet smear had got under his skin.

Birdy had already contacted his Commanding Officer and announced wryly that it had not been his best ever interview.

'I've bought some time,' he said, 'time, as the Old Man put it, to prove I wasn't regressing to my teenage years.'

Birdy admitted that the time was coming for a review of his attachment to the SAS, when he would have to decide whether to resume his naval career, 'assuming I have a career to resume,' he added. We all knew that Birdy was completely divided on the issue. The SAS had become his spiritual home, but he knew that if he was to progress beyond lieutenant commander he would have to go back either to naval flying, or, what was in his eyes even worse, apply to transfer to the Navy's general branch, as his relatives were keen for him to do.

'Haven't you got a spare admiral in the family who can sort this out,' I asked. I meant it as a joke but Birdy took the question seriously. 'No one would ever intervene on my behalf,' he said, 'they wouldn't see it as the right and fair thing to do and I'd agree with them.'

Tim had been on his cell phone more or less continuously since the cowardice accusation, but he had also been half-listening to Birdy.

'I've bought some time too, but I have no idea at the moment what the hell to do with it,' he said. 'The CO at Hereford is basically on my side. He wasn't in Afghanistan at the time, but he does accept my assertion that we were ordered at the last moment to abort the rescue mission. But apparently the MoD is going ape shit. They've been asked by the US Defense Department to launch a formal enquiry. The CO is stalling but it looks as though I've got two weeks at most to marshal my defence. It's going to be a hell of a job because I had no idea I would have anything to defend. The rescue mission didn't fail, it never started, but establishing where the order to abort originated isn't going to be easy at this late stage.'

'Let's get some sleep,' I said, 'and have the rest of the debrief at sea.'

I did manage to get some sleep and anyway I wasn't given much alternative. I lay beside Kate but touched her as little as possible. I wasn't sure how bad her shoulder was but it remained the 'excuse du jour' for fending off any intimacy and Kate was still out of sorts.

'It seems Sandra is very good,' she said when I asked how the Games coverage was going. 'She's taken over completely. I might as well be home in the States.'

'What's the word from Ocean Reports?' I asked.

'The publisher says he wants to wait for an objective assessment.'

'What does that mean?'

'It means that my case is being argued by people he knows are all my close friends. Maxine Herald is a clever bitch, I'll give her that. When it's clear I'm not pregnant, she still has the abortion rumour to play with. Marie may be staying for now, but she will have to leave at some point and I'll be declared the victor in some ridiculous love conflict. Ocean Reports are a pretty priggish bunch. They are going to take a lot of convincing.'

'At least you'll be sailing in a while,' I said.

In answer, I got the first real smile I had seen in days.

'Oh yes,' Kate said, 'thank God for Bouncer.'

I knew Kate would be happy to get back to her natural environment, but I was still taken aback by the extent of the transformation. From the moment she stepped on board the *Nova Scotia*, Kate was a totally different person. Bouncer announced that he would stay close to the helm because of the damage to Kate's shoulder, but Kate would be in command. There was no hint of challenge in his tone. I could see he really wanted to watch how a round-the-world yachtswoman would handle his family boat.

Kate immediately took control. We were all pretty bleary eyed in the dawn half-light, after being driven to the outer harbour in our ridiculous stretch limo.

Kate, by contrast, was fully alert and ordered us all to put on life jackets and made sure they were fitted properly. Everyone on board except Marie was familiar with boats. Most had trained for water-borne operations, even though they had never specialised but only Birdy had much experience of sailing. I was the least experienced. I was comfortable at sea but I had spent only a brief period using boats during my undercover work for SIS.

'First I need to know where everything is,' Kate said.

Bouncer took his cue and showed her the layout. By any standards, the *Nova Scotia* was a beautiful craft. She was a 50-foot wooden ketch, teak built with lovingly-restored brass and bronze fittings.

'We have three sails,' Bouncer said, 'mizzen, mainsail and Genoa. Perkins Diesel engine. We'll have to motor out. There's a narrow channel we have to go through because of Olympic security.'

I followed behind them as Bouncer gave her a running commentary on the boat's features. Kate insisted on knowing every detail, down to which lockers contained the petrol, paint, diesel, flares and gas cylinders.

'Bow thruster?' she asked.

When she saw me looking confused, she explained that the bow-thruster was a small propeller-type device which could be used to move the bow around.

'Yes,' Bouncer said, 'the controls are here,' he pointed to two buttons in the aft cockpit, 'green to move to starboard, red to port.'

Kate smiled. 'We are spoiled.'

She was clearly very impressed with her new charge. The only feature that jarred slightly was a small grey RIB yacht tender, in the water astern, which looked too modern to match the rest of the yacht.

'That was my brother's idea,' Bouncer said apologetically. 'He wanted something a bit faster and snazzier than what we had and Dad let him have it because Davie did most of the work restoring the boat.

'We'll have to tow her,' he added apologetically, 'one of the davits for hoisting the tender aboard is damaged and we haven't had time to repair it.'

Kate inspected the tender and I could see she didn't really approve, but she wasn't going to let anything spoil her pleasure. We were all relieved to be free of the claustrophobia of the past days, but Kate was ecstatic. It was obvious that all her land concerns had been left behind, and I guessed she wouldn't be taking part in any of our briefings.

I suspected also that her mood was secretly helped by the fact that Marie began to feel queasy before we had even left the quayside.

'I'm afraid Marie is into horses not boats,' I whispered as Kate noted her discomfort. 'Oh, she'll be fine,' Kate said cheerfully, but it didn't sound as though she cared much one way or the other. This was her world, not Marie's, and the idea of any competition between the two women had simply dissolved in the sea air.

Birdy stayed ashore to cast off the bow line. Kate gave a five-second burst of the bow thruster so that we were heading out into the main channel, then Birdy dropped the spring lines, cast off the stern warp and jumped aboard, while Tim and Lottery pulled in the four fenders.

Security for the sailing Olympics was indeed tight. We left the harbour under engine power and had to pass through three cordons.

The inner cordon, immediately outside the harbour, consisted of what Bouncer called 'the men in balaclavas you don't argue with.' They weren't actually in balaclavas, but we were checked by four members of the Royal Marines Special Boat Service in a twin-engine RIB. One of them recognised Tim and gave him a discreet wave as we were ushered through to the second cordon. This consisted of police boats and this time Rachel was recognised. There was no wave, but the sergeant in charge of the nearest RIB acknowledged her with a brief smile as we passed out into open water.

The outer, third cordon consisted of assorted private vessels from the local community whose skippers had volunteered their boats and their time for the duration of the Games. Predictably, Bouncer seemed to know everyone and we were given a regal send-off into the open sea.

Bouncer turned the boat into wind and Kate gave the order to raise the mizzen and main sails. I had expected that Kate would want to raise all the sails as soon as we were clear of the cordons, but she explained that Bouncer had briefed her about something called the Portland Race, a challenging and potentially dangerous flow of water off Portland Bill.

'The tide is apparently too strong to sail through the Race, so we're going to stay close to the shore until we get round the Bill,' Kate said.

'Isn't it dangerous to stay so close to the shore in a boat this size? I asked.

Bouncer grinned. 'No, I know these waters well. There are a few fishing pots about, but I'll keep a good look out for them.'

I wanted to stay and chat to Kate but I saw that Marie was crouching in an almost foetal position on the foredeck, and I made my way over to her.

'I feel so useless,' Marie said, as I sat down beside her.

'I'm sorry we couldn't come on horseback,' I said, 'but it's only seahorses round here.'

Marie gave me a wan smile. She was a superb horsewoman and as far as I knew, that was her only sporting interest unless you counted bridge.

'I hate boats,' she said. 'When I came to Weymouth I wasn't expecting to have to go out to sea, but it's not just that,' she added. 'I really did come to Weymouth to try to help and, so far, I've done absolutely nothing except add to the chaos. I tried to get some more information out of my London law contacts, but all their sources could say was that the Vosslers have taken practically a whole floor at the Ritz, and they don't go out or receive visitors, other than the Maxine Herald crowd.'

'This is a new situation for all of us,' I said. 'It's a new kind of conflict and for now they've got was on the run, but we will counter-attack, I promise you.'

'It has to die down eventually, I suppose,' Marie said.

'Even when it does, it's going to take a long time and a lot of effort to restore our reputations,' I said, 'but to be honest, it's Tim I'm most worried about just now. His career could be completely shattered by this. I think Chunk and Birdy and Lottery will be alright. It may take much too long for comfort, but they're survivors. They'll get through somehow. Same with Kate. Whatever happens with Ocean Reports, Kate's track record will keep her inside the sailing community. There will be other expeditions. But Tim is a different matter. Coward is a word that sticks forever, especially in the Armed Forces.'

'Can I say one thing about you?' Marie said. 'It's not about us,' she added quickly, 'I want to give you some legal advice.'

I smiled. 'Please do.'

'I'm serious,' she said. She pointed to the compact Nikon camera bag I had attached to my waist belt. 'Tim told me what that was.'

Inside the camera bag was the catapult which had been my weapon of choice in many difficult situations. I had first been taught to use a slingshot in the desert and over the years I had refined both the weapon and my skill with it. The version in the camera bag was a highly sophisticated slingshot of my own design. It collapsed into a compact metal bar with powerful industrial elastic bands fitted neatly around it, together with a supply of heavy metal ball-bearings for ammunition. I was wearing it for the first time in Weymouth and when Tim had seen it he had said 'Mind you don't take a selfie with that thing.' Marie's reaction was clearly going to be more solemn.

'You're wearing it because you think Ali Omar might show up?' Marie said.

'It's a possibility. The people Omar hired to try to snatch Kate and damage Birdy's helicopter told us he has a personal grudge against me. He may well come after me, or try to get Kate again.

'And Omar is a brute and a killer.'

'Yes indeed.'

'And a fight with him could turn seriously nasty.'

'Oh yes.'

'That's what I thought,' Marie said, 'which is why I want to say something as a lawyer not a lover, sorry ex-lover. I'm not an expert in English law but I'm pretty familiar with the basics.'

'Go on,' I said cautiously, not expecting to like what I was about to hear.

'If Omar can't get you, he'll try to get Kate because you would be mortified if a second woman got hurt because of your intelligence work. It would be your Sarah all over again, wouldn't it?'

'Yes.'

'In effect, there is a feud between you. But this isn't Sicily. British courts don't understand vendettas and we aren't in a war zone. If you fight and he ends up dead, you could face a murder charge, or at best manslaughter. A prosecuting barrister would make mince-meat of a defence based on Omar's past behaviour. Proportionate response is one of the trickiest areas in criminal law.'

'I know that.'

'Yes, but do you really grasp the legal implications?'

'Yes, I do, but if someone like Omar comes after you, you have to fight back.'

'Well remember what I said,' she sighed, 'I'm very fond of you, John, and I'd rather be your lover than your lawyer. Please be careful.'

I knew Marie was right but I wanted to end the conversation before it became too sentimental. I looked around to see if there were any signs of the planned debrief getting started, but everyone was preoccupied. Chunk was amidships and still glued to his cell-phone. He usually hated the intrusion of mobiles into everyday life, so I presumed whatever negotiations were going on with his family had reached a critical stage. I was saved by Rachel who had been talking intently to Tim, but who made her way across the deck to sit down beside Marie.

'Am I interrupting?'

'Of course not. Can I do anything to help?' I asked.

'That's what I came to talk to you about.'

'Anything I can do, I will.'

Rachel smiled. 'That's what Tim said you would say, but I don't want help. That's what I came to explain.'

Marie offered to leave us alone to talk, but Rachel said there was no need.

'Tim told me that your style is to take all the world's problems on your shoulders. He says you will do anything for a friend, that's why you have your magic 'network.' But what I need,' Rachel went on, 'is for you not to try to help me. The Met is a very closed world and fortunately I have my own little network inside it. Everyone on my team knows I wasn't to blame for the collapse of the Finwell case. They'll find ways of filtering that up to the stratosphere, through the right channels, at the right time, and we'll come up with a way of making a public denial stick.'

She laughed. 'I'm having to put up with quite a few tit jokes along the way, but that goes with the territory, I'm afraid.'

'I'm very glad you think you can manage,' I said, 'and a bit relieved too. I know your professional world is different and I'm struggling in my own at the moment.'

I thought yet again about Heather Fenton and how alarming it was how much power social media had given to a woman like her. In Amman, once you got to know her, she became a figure of ridicule and her gossip dismissed as the trivial nonsense. Now that she had gone viral, she could do me lasting damage.

'Just do what you can for Tim,' Rachel said, interrupting my thoughts, 'he really doesn't deserve this.'

'You have my word,' I said, 'I don't know yet what the best way is, but none us will rest easy until the cowardice slur is put to sleep.'

Rachel glanced over my shoulder.

'I think Tim wants us to start the briefing.'

We gathered on the main deck, leaving Bouncer at the wheel with Kate beside him. As I had expected, Kate had no plans to switch her attention away from the sea and take part.

Tim and I tried to run a normal debrief, but it simply didn't work. Even though we were together and clearly ready to co-operate, no-one had the slightest idea of what to do next. I had never seen the network so uncertain. These were some of the most imaginative men I had ever come across, inside the military or out, but on this battle ground we were all floundering. But we could agree on one thing: we had to get MI6 on our side. It was easy to say, but very difficult to do. As soon as the UpstairsBackstairs bile had started pouring out, I had realised that only the intelligence community had the authority and credibility to undermine the new Vossler version of events. On the surface, the CIA was buying it, but there were almost certainly pro-and anti-Vossler factions within the Agency. With Cronin out of action though, it wasn't going to be easy to find out who in the CIA might support us. Which only left MI6 and that in turn meant Virginia, my least favourite potential ally.

Tim put it bluntly and accurately. 'You can bet Six knows for certain it wasn't a sting. They must have done their own investigations even while we were catching Vossler red-handed.'

I had no choice but to admit the doubt that I just couldn't get rid of.

'I'm sure that's right,' I said, 'but they may well have decided yet again Anglo-American cooperation over intelligence is more valuable than our small lives.'

'How do you stand with Virginia, these days? Tim asked.

'To be honest, I've no idea.'

'No surprise there, then,' Lottery said.

'I'll just have to pick the right moment to try to find out,' I said, 'but she may well not have decided yet. Virginia's great skill is waiting to see how the wind is blowing before setting her sails accordingly.'

To cheer the group up a bit, I asked Rachel's permission to tell everyone what she had told me. She nodded and I explained that she was going to solve her own problems.

'I wish someone would solve my problem,' Lottery said grumpily.

Everyone laughed. 'We're all facing career meltdown and international ridicule and you're worried about your girlfriend,' Birdy said. 'Just be grateful you aren't under attack.'

'Fucking typical,' Lottery said, 'sergeants always get neglected until they're needed for some shit job.'

'Don't worry,' Tim said, 'we're all being attacked because of our superior intellect, so you're quite safe.'

'Well if you're so fucking clever, perhaps you can find a way of getting Clara back.'

'Can a woman help?' Rachel said, laughing. 'What have you done so far?'

'I called her early this morning. I thought I'd catch her while she was still in bed and we could have a bit of chit-chat and a quick reconciliation.'

Rachel groaned. 'Maybe the bachelor life would suit you better.'

Lottery was smiling now and I knew he was keeping up the banter to stop the general mood from becoming irretrievably gloomy.

He was thinking up a reply when Chunk came over and sat down with the group, his cell-phone now out of sight for the first time since we had come aboard.

'Family OK?' I said, not expecting a detailed answer.

'I have some good news, potentially,' Chunk said.

'Your brother recovering?'

'No, it's nothing to do with my family. All my phoning has been about Tim.'

'And you have good news? I prompted, surprised.

'I think so, yes, but there's a snag, which I'll come to in a minute.'

Chunk sat back and made himself comfortable leaning against the mast.

'I've been calling all my friends in US Special Forces and I think I've found out what's been going on. I've got confirmation that you had orders not to attack,' Chunk turned to Tim, 'not that I ever doubted it, but the background is particularly complicated. The girl was called Veronica Malone, was she not?'

Tim nodded.

'Well it seems that behind the scenes, her father, Ed Malone, a very wealthy businessman who lives in Kansas City, was conducting negotiations with the kidnappers. It was all unofficial because the US authorities didn't want to be upfront about paying ransom. The rescue operation had already been planned but was put on hold at the father's request.

'The Taliban asked for a huge sum. The father reluctantly agreed but said he needed time to raise the money. Meanwhile, the Taliban got wind of the rescue op, panicked, killed the girl and got the hell out.

'Ever since, the father has been torturing himself for not raising the money fast enough and blaming himself for his daughter's death.'

'So what did the Vosslers do?' I said.

'When the Vosslers got wind of the story, Ivan went to see the father and told him that Veronica's death wasn't his fault. He said Special Forces knew the Taliban didn't plan to honour the deal and had decided to go ahead with the rescue. Ivan told Malone it was to be a joint US-British op but the Brits – led by Tim – bottled it and didn't turn up.'

'There must be scores of people who know that isn't true,' Tim said.

'Yes, I'm sure there are, but Ivan has managed to sell their version to a key player, General Scott Hartnett, who is an old West Point classmate of his and a very influential figure in Washington. It's Hartnett who persuaded the Defense Department to ask MoD for an inquiry.'

'That doesn't sound like good news to me,' Tim said. 'How on earth are we going to persuade Hartnett that Vossler is lying?'

'Well I have good and bad news here,' Chunk said. 'The good news is that Hartnett is known to be a man of honour and integrity and I gather he was a bit suspicious of Ivan, even though they are West Point buddies. If we can find the right person to approach him, I think we could get the matter put right.'

'But how do we find the right person?' Tim said, 'I've only got two weeks, if that.'

'Well that's the bad news,' Chunk said, 'turning to me. There is a perfect person – your former father-in-law, General Adrian Standish. Hartnett and Standish served together in NATO, in fact they had adjacent offices at SHAPE headquarters in Belgium. Standish is a man of integrity also. I think he could be persuaded to intervene, if John is willing to make the approach.'

'Of course I'm willing to try,' I said, 'but he hates my guts. I'm not even sure he'd be willing to speak to me.'

'I think we have to make the attempt,' Chunk said.

'Then I'll certainly try,' I said.

I said it as confidently as I could, but I could imagine only too well how it could go horribly wrong. Standish was retired now and lived a fairly reclusive life with his wife Patricia in their country home in rural Kent. If he agreed to see me at all, it would probably be at his home, which would mean his wife would be there, and she hated me even more than the general did.

They both blamed me for Sarah's death and Patricia's hatred was almost pathological. I had never had chance to put my side of the story.

As John Cartwright I had been barred from approaching anyone from my old life, and since resuming life as John Saxon, I was still summoning up the courage.

'Good,' Chunk said, 'I'll call Standish and try to set something up.'

At that point Kate came over and I could see she was getting impatient that no-one seemed to be interested our surroundings.

'Why don't you leave all this for a while,' she suggested, 'we're past the Race now and we are heading for the open sea. Time to un-furl the Genoa and do some real sailing.'

For almost two hours we did just that, and everyone tried to put their troubles aside, except for Marie who was in a state of complete misery. I offered to ask Kate to turn back, but Marie urged me not to. 'This is the first day Kate's enjoyed since we got here and I can't spoil it.'

She was right of course and it was a truly glorious afternoon. We had come about and were heading back towards Weymouth. Bouncer said we had two hours of slack water, so we could sail back through the Race then stay on the outskirts of the Olympic sailing venues and watch the competition, even though we would be forced to keep a good distance away. We would not be able to see any of the manoeuvring or study race techniques, but the spectacle of Weymouth Bay dotted with a hundred yachts was a splendid sight in itself, and for the first time, we would actually be able to feel as though we were part of the Games, if only a very detached one.

After a while, I left Marie and stood by the mizzen mast, apart from the others. I wanted to think about how to approach my father-in-law and, unconsciously, I had already started drafting words in my head that might break down the barrier between us.

Then suddenly I heard a shout and felt a violent shock on my left side which knocked me to the deck. It was Kate. She had body-charged me violently and sent us both crashing down. I wasn't hurt but Kate was wincing with pain after lunging her damaged shoulder directly into me. In the same instant, I saw why. Quivering in the mast above us, exactly at the height my back would have been, was a crossbow bolt.

The whole boat came frantically to life. Everyone on board knew what a crossbow bolt meant. Ali Omar was attacking. He was as skilled with the crossbow as I was with the catapult and I knew I dare not move, as a second bolt would follow the minute I showed my head.

He had to be close. Even with Omar's skill, the crossbow was only accurate at about fifty yards, allowing for the wind and the movement of the sea.

Lying next to me, Kate was clearly in agony. I couldn't assess from that angle how badly she'd been hurt, but the bulwark was very low and if we started to move, I knew Omar would take his next shot.

'Lie still,' I said, 'stay exactly where you are,' then I shouted, 'anyone got sight of him?'

It was Bouncer who answered. He was crouching down in the cockpit, using the wheel to protect himself.

'He's in a small RIB, just off the bow.'

'Is he alone?'

'Yes. He's re-arming the crossbow and about to take another shot.'

'Everybody in cover?' I shouted again.

The answers came in quick succession. Everyone was in cover.

He won't fire again unless he sees a target,' I shouted. 'It's me he's after, or Kate.'

But I was wrong. Omar did fire again and this time, the target wasn't Kate or me, it was the boat. The bolt was a fire arrow, but a modern version, with an explosive incendiary head. It struck the *Nova Scotia* amidships and fire broke out instantly.

'Extinguishers near the engine compartment,' Bouncer shouted.

Kate started to struggle to her feet, but I held her down.

'That's what he wants. He wants to flush us into the open.'

'Any weapons on board? I shouted to Bouncer.

'No'

'Flares?'

'Yes. In the port forward locker.'

'Stay there,' I hissed at Kate, 'the gang will fight the fire.'

We were under attack once more, but this time we weren't in disarray.

No-one needed to give anyone orders. Chunk had the best visibility apart from Bouncer and he took command, directing by hand gestures.

Lottery, who was nearest, crawled at astonishing speed to get a flare. Manoeuvring on his back, Tim grabbed one fire extinguisher and Rachel got the second. This was the network's kind of fighting. Everyone knew the moves and had no problem assessing what Omar would do next. I stayed with Kate and held her tightly. She didn't know the moves, even though it was her sea eyes that had probably saved my life. Lottery crawled back on deck and his return of fire was textbook. He lifted his head above the bulwark for a fraction of second, withdrew it, moved two feet to the right, popped up again and fired a flare.

It didn't hit Omar or his boat but it was close enough.

'He's heading off,' Chunk shouted.

That was my cue.

'I'm going after him.'

I eased myself off Kate.

'Are you OK?'

I could see she was fighting the pain, but she didn't hesitate.

'Don't worry about me, just get the bastard.'

I ran to the aft deck and asked Bouncer to help me get into the RIB. Bouncer hauled on the line to bring the tiny boat alongside under the stern. Tim ran to join me and made signs that he was coming with me.

'No,' I said, 'you're in enough trouble. Omar is mine.'

I jumped in and started the engine before he had chance to argue. The chase was on!

13

I saw straightaway I was not going to catch Omar on the water. The best I could hope for was to keep him in sight until he reached the shore. His boat was doing a good 10 knots faster than my tender, but he was veering in a semicircle as though he was not sure of his way, so I did have a chance.

Fairly soon it became obvious there was only one place he could land, a small cove with a shingle beach enclosed by steep wooded cliffs. When he beached his RIB, I was still too far offshore to make out exactly where he was going and by the time I crashed my tender onto the shingle he had disappeared. The beach wasn't crowded but there were a few swimmers and sunbathers and a handful of families in front of the beach huts at the foot of the cliff. Omar had obviously landed with the same lack of finesse I had, and a young couple with two children were public-spiritedly trying to drag his boat up the beach to stop it drifting out to sea. My tender was lighter and though my arrival wasn't elegant, I did slide more firmly onto the stones.

I jumped ashore and shouted to the man manoeuvring Omar's boat, 'which way did he go?' The man didn't answer and I could see he was nervous about what he was getting into. I reached for my wallet and waved my all-purpose fake ID, which was impressive if not examined too closely. The man looked at me and at the ID and then at my boat. I realised for the first time that it was called the 'Flirty Mary' which did take the edge off any official status.

'Which way did he go?' I snapped, 'I need to know right now.'

I used a voice that was fierce enough to make up for the name of my boat and this time my authority wasn't questioned. The father pointed towards the cliff and at first I thought he meant Omar had gone into one of the beach huts.

'Which one? I said.

'No, not the huts, the little path at the side.'

'Was he carrying a weapon, a crossbow?'

'He had a black bag, a big one.'

The older of the two boys who had been listening said, 'there was a crossbow inside, I saw it, the bag was torn.'

'Thanks very much,' I said and sprinted towards the wooded section of the cliff.

There was an easier way from the beach to the top of the cliff, a broad path with sets of steps at intervals, which wound its way up to what looked like part of a ruined castle. There were at least ten people making their way down that path and Omar would have been too conspicuous. He was a very easy man to remember. Omar was barely five feet tall but incredibly powerfully built. He had been rejected by the US Special Forces because of his height and had spent a lifetime compensating, becoming a skilled gymnast, wrestler and weightlifter, as well as a professional killer. If the boy on the beach could spot the crossbow that easily, then he was going to have a lot of trouble keeping out of sight.

Omar had figured that out for himself. As soon as I went into the wood I found the crossbow. He had made a token attempt to conceal it - I knew he valued his crossbows, which he customised with great care - but he clearly valued speed more and I easily spotted the bag in a thicket of brambles and undergrowth.

I was glad he had shed the weapon, but he could now move faster than I could in this kind of terrain. Climbing the cliff through the undergrowth was hard going. The path narrowed very quickly and was so overgrown that I doubted anyone but a naturalist interested in plant species would use it. It took me several minutes pick my way through the rough scrub and brambles, and I was scratched and sweating by the time I reached the top.

If Omar had a car waiting for him, I had no chance of catching him, but I didn't think he had set out from this cove. He had given the impression of looking desperately for somewhere to land, which meant he would have to summon some kind of transport. My best hope was that it would take some time to agree on the exact pickup point, as Omar wouldn't know the area. He might be super-organised and using GPS co-ordinates but I doubted it. That wasn't Omar's style. Much more likely was a phone call to a buddy and a scramble to agree a rendezvous point.

The path we had both climbed came out behind two very elegant houses with extensive sunken, walled gardens. A narrow lane with high overgrown walls divided the houses from a small local museum which was holding some kind of open event. People were milling around the museum entrance and a long queue for ice creams and drinks stretched out into the main road. Omar would be highly conspicuous if he stood near there. That left him two choices: either he could hide somewhere and wait for a vehicle to pick him up or he could walk down the road until he found somewhere quieter.

My instinct was that Omar would go for concealment. If I were in Omar's place and didn't know the area, I would make use of the obvious landmark. I would say to the pickup driver, 'find the Portland museum, drive slowly past it so I know you've arrived, then go on round the curve, park and wait till it's safe for me to find you.' It turned out I was right.

I looked around for places where he could hide and watch the road. The most likely spots were inside the wall around the sunken garden of the biggest of the two houses near the museum. The house was a stone structure in the typical Portland style, but modernised with solar panels and a tastefully-designed veranda and decking. The veranda overlooked an elegant garden. Near the veranda was a carefully tended lawn, divided by a path which led to a painted wooden bridge. On the other side of the bridge, the garden became wilder with several varieties of pine tree among boulders, which had probably been brought from the neighbouring quarries.

Along the outer wall there was a walkway. That was too obvious a place to stand and watch the road but there were other potential observation points which could not be seen from the house. It didn't take long to spot Omar. He had not been very original. Along one section of the wall was a series of ornamental slots designed to create the effect of a battlement. Omar had chosen one where he had a good view of the road but was out of sight of the house, and he had simply counted on the garden remaining empty. He was crouched down, talking on his cell-phone.

I estimated I could get within fifty metres of him without being seen, and from there the terrain was smooth. A few strides and a lunge and I could be at close quarters. It was exactly the kind of confrontation I was hoping for. In the kind of mental state I was in, there was no way Omar would get the better of me. This would be our last fight and I didn't intend to lose it. I remembered Marie's warning that I must not kill him but I wouldn't need to. I wanted him re-arrested, but not before I had hurt him badly enough for him to remember me in his nightmares.

I moved quietly round to the end of the walkway, took a deep breath, then sprinted down it, intending to be on him before he even realised he was under attack. It was a sound enough tactic but I under-estimated Omar's speed and agility. Omar was a superb athlete and as agile as a monkey. Instead of trying to grapple with me, he did a side flip that was almost a somersault and before I could complete my lunge he was off the walkway and running over the bridge and onto the lawn.

I had been so near, but now the situation turned horribly wrong. At the very moment Omar made his escape, an elegantly-dressed young woman in her early twenties came out onto the veranda. As she saw Omar running towards her, she tried to get back into the house but Omar was too quick for her and for me. Before I was over the bridge, Omar had his arm round her neck and the Sado at her throat.

The Sado was his personal weapon. He had designed it and refined it over the years. It was his trademark, a weapon for close combat and for intimidation and torture. It was shaped like a knuckle-duster but the forward surface was edged with razor wire which could virtually shred an opponent's face. Inside the lead-weighted hand-piece was a powerful Taser.

I loaded the catapult but didn't raise it. Omar knew I didn't need to. I could lift my arm and fire in a single movement, just as I knew he could maim the young woman in a split second. The stand-off was total.

I studied the position, looking for a way to get an edge. Omar's stance was awkward because the woman was tall and he was having to drag her down towards him to keep the Sado close to her neck. He was looking straight at me and smiling. With his left hand, he started to feel the woman's groin.

He didn't speak. He just mouthed 'Not as good as Sarah.'

Very calmly I said, 'Go for it, I'm about to blind you,' and raised the catapult.

I got the reaction I wanted. Instinctively, he moved his head behind the woman's body. Before he had time to adjust his position, I fired a ball at his elbow. I missed the joint but hit his upper arm. The pain must have been excruciating, but Omar didn't drop the Sado or cry out. When the woman felt his grip relax, she found the courage to try to push him away but she couldn't budge him. I had been up against Omar in close combat and I knew the woman would feel as though she was pushing against a truck tyre. I prayed even Omar had the sense to see that if he injured the woman, he would achieve nothing, and guessed what he would do next. He would try the Taser.

From behind the woman he couldn't see me properly, but when he showed himself, I calculated I would have a split second to fire again before he had a chance to put me out of action. I was wrong. Omar decided flight was the better option.

I realised afterwards that I'd probably damaged his arm enough to make him afraid it would affect his aim. Suddenly, he pushed the woman towards me and ran for the wall nearest to the museum. I should have fired immediately, but I made the mistake of looking towards the woman to make sure Omar hadn't cut her. She was writhing on the ground but there was no sign of blood, but in those few seconds, Omar was already vaulting over the top of the stonework. When I did fire, I was lucky to hit him on the shoulder. It was another viciously painful blow, but not disabling.

I shouted to the woman to call the police and sprinted after Omar. When I got to the top of the wall, I expected to see Omar forcing his way through the little crowd wandering about in the lane below, but there was no sign of him.

Then I saw him. He was keeping high, running along the top of a stretch of ruined wall that led to the castle-like building at the top of the cliff. I could see why he had chosen that way. He was much more nimble and agile than I was and I had damaged his arm and shoulder, but not his legs. I climbed onto the wall and started to run along the uneven stonework. I had always been good enough on assault courses, but I wasn't in Omar's league. I knew he spent hours every week straining for perfection in the gym, in every discipline - balance, strength and tumbling. Within minutes, he was out of sight. If he could maintain that speed, he would reach the castle long before I could, then leap onto the main path down to the beach and be within reach of his boat.

I decided my best chance was to jump down onto the regular path and try and cut him off. It wasn't a great chance, but I hadn't a hope of matching his acrobatic skills at this height.

I scrambled down in two stages and had just reached the ground and started to run when I heard a piercing scream followed by a loud thud. It had to be Omar, but I had no idea what had happened. I kept on running and when the sea came into view, I saw Omar. He was lying - very obviously dead – at the foot of the tower that formed the corner of the ruined castle. Two men were running up from the beach towards him and they got there before I did.

'What happened?' I shouted as I ran down the path.

'Don't know,' one of the men said. 'I saw him fall, but I've no idea what caused it.'

I looked down at Omar's body and felt suddenly cold. There was no feeling of triumph or relief at the death of a man I despised and detested, a man who had caused me so much grief. Instead, all I could think of was Marie's words, 'John you mustn't kill him. Whatever he's done to you in the past won't make it self-defence.'

The reality was that I hadn't even seen his death, but could I prove it? If there was an autopsy – and there surely would be – they would find two huge bruises on his arm and shoulder. They would probably establish they were caused before death, but not necessarily exactly when. The woman at the house had seen me using the catapult but she had been far too terrified to see whether I had hit him, especially the second time when she had been writhing on the ground. Anyone who knew Omar could testify to his athletic and gymnastic skills, so why should he fall off the castle tower? One obvious answer that would occur to the police was because he had been hit by a catapult ball, fired by the man chasing him.

I waited beside the body for the police to arrive and it was Frampton who was in charge.

Before I began to give him my account, I asked him what had happened on board the *Nova Scotia*.

'They put the fire out very efficiently and got help pretty quickly. A police RIB got there first, then the lifeboat. There wasn't much damage.'

'And no-one was injured?'

'Kate's shoulder isn't in great shape. They've taken her to the specialist unit at Dorchester hospital. I gather she saved your life.'

'Yes, she did.'

'And cleared the way for you to settle scores with this fellow,' Frampton said, nodding towards Omar.

'I never got the chance. He was way ahead of me when he fell.'

I gave him a detailed account, starting with the chase by boat and the landing at the cove.

Frampton listened then pointed to my catapult.

'When he fell, he was really out of range of that? It's a pretty powerful weapon.'

I should have known Frampton would come straight to the point.

'I give you my word,' I said, 'I had no part in his death.'

'Let's hope your word stands up in court,' he said.

I knew how shaky my position was. Frampton had never been hostile, but others certainly would be.

When the ambulance arrived, it couldn't get any nearer than the museum and two paramedics stretchered the body up the long path, watched by a crowd of fascinated tourists, many with the inevitable mobile phones to record the event.

'Your friends aren't far away,' Frampton said. 'The lifeboat brought them ashore and Kate and Bouncer are bringing the yacht back. They followed me down. I told them to wait at the New Inn, just up the road.

When we reached the pub, I found Tim, Rachel, Birdy and Lottery gathered in a small back room. They were all looking solemn and I didn't have to ask why. What did surprise me was Tim's first question.

'Where did you hit him? It must have been a great shot to knock him right off the cliff.'

I couldn't believe an old friend could be so stupidly indiscreet. I knew Frampton was, in principle, on our side, but I was quite sure he wouldn't falsify evidence to help me.

'I didn't fire any shots.'

Tim grinned. 'That's OK then. They won't find any bruises on the body.'

What the hell was going on? Frampton was listening intently and the others were doing nothing to help me.

Then suddenly they all burst out laughing, including Frampton.

'Don't worry old buddy, we've watched the whole thing,' Tim said. 'Jay had a drone up. He's got it all on record.'

'What!'

I called Jay straightaway,' Tim said. 'He was already up here playing with his toys. He had you on camera as soon as you hit the beach.'

Lottery laughed. 'You need some more target practice. That shot on the elbow was great but you could have stopped him getting over the wall. That was careless.'

'So how did he fall?'

'Trying to be too clever. He ran along the castle wall too fast. A little piece of stone crumbled and down he went. You were still at the top of the alleyway. If he hadn't fallen, he'd probably have made it.'

I turned to Frampton. 'And you've seen all this?'

Frampton was smiling. 'Yes. I've seen the whole chase. We'll interview the woman he took hostage. You're in the clear.'

But of course, it wasn't that simple! The truth had no influence on the story that began running on UpstairsBackstairs soon after we were back on board the *Jessica*.

I had just decided to go to Dorchester to see Kate when a news stream opened with the headline: **Duel at the Castle - John Saxon kills his wife's ex-lover in cliff top showdown.** In the clear with the police I might be, but the story contained every detail from my worst nightmare. It had been written by someone who knew Portland far better than I did and even the history of the area had been used to twist the knife. I learned that the bay where we had both landed was called Church Ope Cove. Ope it seemed was the local word for a narrow passageway and the building Omar had fallen from was called Rufus Castle, built, it was pointed out with appropriate irony, in Saxon times. The story described a chase from the sea to the cliff top, but there was no mention of Omar's attempt to take the woman hostage. Instead, it described a spectacular 'duel on the battlements' ending with me firing a shot with the catapult which had sent Omar, the man I hated most in the world, plummeting to his death. The story even pointed out that my attack on Omar was in line with local custom of using stones to repel invaders from the sea but, it said, this was no historical re-enactment - it was cold-blooded murder.

The story was accompanied by photographs of the cove and the castle and there were also photographs of Omar and me. These were not taken at the scene but were archive shots, clearly chosen to emphasise my bulky frame and Omar's tiny stature to hint at an extra layer of ruthless bullying.

More background followed, rehearsing yet again the lies about Sarah's alleged affair with Omar and my determination to seek revenge.

Frampton was with us as we watched the story run.

'They're damned clever, you have to give them that,' he said, 'if it hadn't been for that drone footage, that would have been a very plausible story.'

'It's still a plausible story,' I said, 'and it's going to take a lot of unpicking. You know what's going to happen. If we put the drone footage online, they're going to say it's edited and rigged to hide the truth. Anyway, just having the drone is going to get Jay into trouble.'

'Jay's not going to mind that,' Tim said, 'but you're right. If you really had killed him, we could have doctored the tape to make it look as though you weren't anywhere near.'

I was just mulling that cheerful thought when we got two more bits of bad news. First, a phone call told us that Kate was being kept in hospital and would need surgery. She had been sedated and would not be able to receive visitors until after the operation. Then Cayman turned up and announced that a breakthrough she had been working towards had fallen through because of the Vossler press conference.

'The *Times* Bureau in Rome had lined up an interview for me with your Italian intelligence general,' she said. 'It seems he's planning to go into politics and was willing to distance himself from Ray Vossler and tell the truth about what happened in Rome. But he's changed his mind now that it looks as though Vossler might turn out to be one of the good guys. We might still get something out of him, but not until you manage to scotch this sting story.'

By this time, social media was excelling itself. A Twitter feed was running with the tag @castleduel. The mainstream media was picking up bits of the story, occasionally adding the odd prefix 'alleged' here and there. We sat around disconsolately for a while discussing non-existent options when Chunk arrived. We didn't need to brief him. He had not been with the others while I was chasing Omar around Portland but Tim had kept him up to date by phone. Once again, we had assumed wrongly that he was occupying himself with family affairs.

'You are going to have to drop everything, John,' he said, 'I've arranged for you to see your father-in-law and it has to be tomorrow.'

14

In the Tiger Moth, Cayman was certainly no Kate. She had agreed to come with me to Kent but she was no fan of open cockpit flying. The best you could say was that she took it stoically. She didn't talk much or respond when I pointed out the landmarks we were flying over, and there was a lot of quiet gripping of the cockpit sides, but I was very glad she was there.

Her coming had been Chunk's idea. He suggested that having an American reporter there would underline the fact that I was going to talk to my former father-in-law about Tim, not just to try to put right the family rift.

Chunk had added politely that it would be a bonus if I could begin some kind of reconciliation, but we both knew that if I could even get the general to talk to me civilly that would be bonus enough.

We reached the general's home just before noon. It was a beautiful 16th century house, built of Kentish blue brick with a long, tiled catslide roof. It had begun life as one of the farms on the estate of Lord Astor, the owner of Hever Castle, but the general had developed it into a comfortable, spacious country home. We landed on what was referred to as Willow Field, where Standish and his wife exercised and trained their horses. The outbuildings consisted of a stable block and a huge barn that had been converted into a garage for three cars.

When we landed I heard Cayman utter a quiet 'Thank God' as I helped her out of the cockpit. There was no sign of anyone coming to meet us and I assumed we would be expected to make our own way to the house, as I had done several times before with Sarah. As we crossed the field and climbed over the style into the small orchard, I saw Sarah's sister, Hannah, running towards us. She had always been friendly towards me, but I hadn't seen or spoken to her since Sarah's death and I had no idea what kind of reception I would get.

As she approached, she held up her hand to stop us coming closer to the house and I thought she had been sent to turn us away.

'We need to talk,' she said, 'let's stay here for a while and I'll tell you what's going on.'

I introduced Cayman and explained why she was with me. Hannah shook hands then turned directly to me.

'Mum and Dad are having the row to end all rows,' she said. 'It's not looking good. Mum only found out this morning that you were coming and she went ballistic. Dad said you were here to discuss a military matter, but Mum said she would leave him if he let you into the house.'

'Hannah, I have to see him,' I said, 'the career of a very fine soldier is at stake.'

'You mean Sergeant Major Overton.'

'You've been following everything on line?'

'Yes.'

I decided to take a gamble.

'You know it's all lies,' I said.

Hannah didn't hesitate.

'Of course I do, John.'

'How do you know?' Cayman interrupted. 'Do you know Heather Fenton?'

'No, but I know my sister. She would never in a million years hook up with someone like this Ali Omar, and she'd never put up with the kind of shit John is supposed to have got up to. It's obviously all made up.'

'But your mother doesn't think so,' Cayman said.

Hannah smiled but without humour. 'Mum thinks a troll is some kind of Scandinavian elf. She hasn't a clue about the internet or social networking. All she knows is that the reputation of a daughter she loved very much is being trashed in a way she couldn't have begun to imagine. She's pretty near a breakdown.'

'So you think we should leave?' I said hesitantly.

'No, not yet. Dad's trying to calm her down. You're not exactly his favourite son-in-law, but if he didn't think there was some point in your being here, he would never have agreed to see you.'

'What do you suggest?'

'Why don't you wait in the garden over by the summer house. That way they can see you're there and Dad will either come or he won't.' She smiled for the first time. 'Someone may pour boiling oil on you from the battlements but I'm sure you're willing to take the risk.'

She looked at her watch. 'I have to go. I'd stay if I thought it would do any good, but I think it would only make it more complicated.'

'Thanks Hannah,' I said, 'I'm very grateful.'

'Be patient,' she said, 'there's a good chance Dad will succeed. After all, he is a general.'

When Hannah had gone, we made our way through the orchard and into the rose garden at the back of the house. There was a small bench in the shade under some trees where we sat looking for any signs of movement.

At first, there was none, then the general appeared at the door of the sunroom, a conservatory that had been added to the original building. Standish was a central-casting general – tall and lean, with a ramrod back and iron grey hair, but there was much more to him than appearance and bearing. As an officer, he didn't have the kind of flair that Chunk had, but he was reliable and brave and much respected by his men. He had served with distinction in Northern Ireland and won a DSO in Kosovo and before his retirement had gone on to key staff positions in NATO and the Ministry of Defence.

We got up and met him halfway across the garden. I introduced Cayman and, as we shook hands and exchanged the formalities, I saw that Chunk had been right - having a third party there made it much easier to avoid any confrontation. Standish led us into the sunroom but before we had chance to settle down in the comfortable armchairs, Patricia Standish burst in and any illusion of formality was immediately shattered.

'I am not having him here, Adrian,' she shouted, 'get him out of the house.'

Without waiting for an answer she turned directly to me.

'Just go,' she said, 'I can't bear to set eyes on you.'

'Patricia, I'm really sorry but I had to come,' I said, 'the career of a very fine soldier is at stake.'

'I suppose that's somebody else's life you ruined,' she responded coldly, 'you seem to have a great talent for that.'

At this point, Cayman intervened. 'General Standish, you might prefer to have this part of the discussion in private. Perhaps I should go into the garden for a while.'

'And who the hell are you?' Patricia snapped, 'another of John's women, the ones we're reading about day after day on the Internet.'

'Ms Cayman is a *New York Times* reporter,' Standish said.

'Here to write more lies, I suppose.'

'Patricia,' I said, 'there is not a single word of truth in anything that is running on the Internet. You have my word.'

'You mean the word of an officer and a gentleman, neither of which you are. I suppose you're going to tell me that Sarah was happy with you. Well, let me tell you something. When you were here together for the wedding, my daughter was as happy as I'd ever seen her, and when she came home from Amman I have never known her so miserable and distraught. That was what you did to her.'

Patricia began to sob uncontrollably and ran from the room.

The general hurried after her and was gone for almost a quarter of an hour. Cayman and I waited, unsure whether he would return. When he did come back, his face was drawn but his voice was calm.

'I'd rather you hadn't seen that,' he said, 'but I'm sure you understand. I know you didn't come here to talk about family matters, but we obviously have no choice. I'll listen to what you have to say and discuss it later with Patricia.'

He sat down and indicated that we should sit opposite.

I knew I had to choose my words very carefully if I was to have any chance of getting Standish to help Tim.

'I know how unhappy Sarah was in Amman,' I began, 'and my only defence is that the life we led there was not of my choosing. My transfer from the army to MI6 was an order, not a request. I'm sure you know that.'

Standish nodded but didn't comment.

'The lifestyle we created in Jordan was planned almost down to the last detail by my intelligence masters,' I said. 'I was put in Amman as a magnet to attract and befriend the kind of people Sarah detested and who, I should mention, I detested also. My other role was to make undercover trips into Iraq, Syria and Lebanon, which meant that Sarah was alone for much of the time. But you must understand this, all the stuff you are reading now about what went on in Amman is a tissue of lies deliberately woven to discredit me, for various political and intelligence reasons. To my knowledge, Sarah never had any affairs, either in Amman or in Rome and neither did I. There were no orgies at our house and Susan al-Maliki was my bridge partner, nothing more. I needed access to a certain group of people in the Amman country club; Sarah didn't want to get involved, so Susan became my conduit.'

As I talked, I could see that Standish was listening intently and weighing every word.

'The trip to Rome with Sarah was, in part, an attempt at reconciliation. We had been discussing the possibility of my leaving SIS despite the relentless pressure I faced to remain an intelligence officer. My plan was to complete the investigation into Ray Vossler's corruption and then request that I be transferred back to the army.'

Standish spoke for the first time. 'Did you really want that?'

'To be absolutely honest, no I didn't. I believed I was doing a good job in the Middle East and I thought I was likely to make a very average regimental officer. I also thought my request would probably be refused anyway and I would end up with no career of any kind. However, I was increasingly concerned about Sarah's state of mind and I wasn't prepared to go on seeing her suffer the way she was.'

I looked straight at Standish. 'My understanding, Sir, is that Sarah asked you whether you could help me get a transfer back to the army.'

Standish didn't answer straightaway and I knew how difficult the question was for him.

'Yes, it's true Sarah told me that you and she were trying to work out a reconciliation,' he said finally, 'and she asked my help to get you back into your regiment.'

'And what did you say?'

I knew we had reached the difficult moment.

'I told Sarah what everyone knew: that you were the most valuable and effective intelligence asset we have had in the Middle East and that returning you to a role as run-of-the-mill officer in London would be a terrible loss.

'I never told Patricia. After Sarah died in such terrible circumstances there was no point. I knew about the deal you were forced to make with SIS, but there was nothing I could do to help. I didn't believe any of the lies about Sarah any more than you did, but I couldn't disprove anything, so I remained silent.

Standish looked sternly at me.

'May I have your assurance, John, your absolute assurance, that all these stories currently running on UpstairsBackstairs, and everything else this Heather Fenton is saying is untrue?'

I spoke solemnly and carefully, with all the respect due to his rank.

'You have my word, Sir, that there is not a word of truth in any of it. Sarah was deeply unhappy, but I repeat, she never had any affairs and neither did I. As I explained, many thoroughly undesirable people came to our house, but I always did my utmost to protect Sarah from them, and nor was I never unfaithful to her when I was undercover outside Jordan. Sarah knew that. What she wanted, quite simply, was to get back to the kind of military life she had grown up in and had loved. I'm only sorry I could never achieve it.'

'I'm relieved, John,' he said. 'All that needed saying, and should have been said long ago. Now let's talk about Sergeant Major Overton.'

On cue, Cayman took out her iPhone and switched on its recorder.

I spoke concisely in measured language, slipping automatically into the style of a military report. I started with the overall picture before coming to Tim's problem. I explained that the Vossler group had decided to rally behind Ray Vossler and were running a very professional political and media campaign to get him freed. The main thrust, I explained, was to claim that the terrorist attack on London had been planned by the Iranians and that Vossler had intervened as a sting operation. They had, quite simply, turned the facts on their head. I went on to explain how individual attacks had been launched on all the members of my so-called network, starting with me personally.

I went over the rumours about me and Kate, my alleged plan to sue MI6, Kate's pregnancy, our plan to marry and my so-called dalliance with Marie – all of which were designed to unleash on us continuous press and social media harassment while at the same time depriving Kate of sponsorship for next sailing expedition. My alleged dissolute behaviour in Amman, I said, was part of a much bigger and more comprehensive character assassination.

Next, I gave the general the details of the vandalisation of Birdy's helicopter, which was designed to make him appear irresponsible in the eyes of the Navy. As I went on to describe the attempt to discredit Rachel by having her blamed for the collapse of the Finwell trial, I could see I had the general's absolute attention. I mentioned the distortion of

Chunk's family problems and their implication for his army career, and I even made a passing joke of the fact that only Lottery had been missed out and that he was quite miffed about it.

'These attacks on us as individuals are meant to disrupt the network and break its cohesion. Just when we need to be working as a team, we are all being deliberately distracted.'

'Is it working?' the general asked.

'To some degree, yes, I admitted, 'mainly because it's taking a great deal of time for each of us to gather the evidence to counter the false claims.'

I explained about the fanciful version of my duel with Ali Omar and the totally false allegation that I had caused his death with a shot from the catapult. I told him about the drone evidence and explained that though I was safe legally, as Inspector Frampton had seen the original drone tape, I would still have great difficulty countering the online allegations, as I could easily be accused of doctoring the tape to take out the incriminating bits.

'It's a new kind of warfare, Sir,' I said. 'We're having a lot of trouble devising a battle plan. I'm confident that we will win in the end, but it will take time and I'm most concerned about Sergeant Major Overton. I don't need to tell you, Sir, that even a whiff of cowardice can ruin the best soldier permanently. What we must avoid at all costs is a long-running debate about whether or not Tim failed in his duty. Even if he is exonerated at an enquiry, there will always be lingering doubts.'

Standish nodded. 'Let me see if I have got the allegation straight in my mind,' he said. 'There was to be a joint US – British special forces operation to free a young female aid worker who had been taken hostage in Afghanistan. The charge against Overton is that he considered the operation too dangerous and failed to turn up, leading to the death of the hostage at the hands of the Taliban.'

'What actually happened, Sir, was that secret negotiations were going on for her release, I said. 'They were haggling over the amount of the ransom. The father said he needed more time to raise the money and asked for the operation to be delayed. The Taliban got wind of the rescue operation, killed the girl, and disappeared. The father has been in a state of deep depression, blaming himself for his daughter's death. The

Vosslers have managed to plant the idea that it was not really his fault and that the delay was caused by the non-appearance of Tim's unit.'

'And what specifically do you want me to do?' Standish asked.

'Ivan Vossler and the girl's father have persuaded General Scott Hartnett to get the US Defense Department to ask the MoD to hold a formal inquiry. I understand that you know Hartnett well. I am hoping you would be willing to intervene.'

Standish thought for a moment.

'What you have told me coincides with my understanding of Sergeant Major Overton's conduct,' he said, 'I've spoken to his CO at Hereford and he is completely convinced that the allegation is false. He told me that he regarded Overton as the best squadron sergeant major he had ever come across.'

'So you will help?'

'Of course. I'll do everything I can, but we have to be careful. I like Scotty. He's a decent sort of chap and we got on well in NATO but he does have political ambitions.'

There was a tiny edge of distaste in Standish's voice. I knew he had no such ambitions and didn't have much respect for military colleagues who did.

'Ivan Vossler is a powerful friend to have in Washington if you see your future in politics. I shall need to tread carefully. As far as I can see, thanks to their concerted social media campaign, the Vosslers are riding high at the moment. How soon do you think you'll be able to start turning the tables?'

'I honestly can't say,' I said. 'What we need most is support from MI6. They must know it wasn't a sting operation. It's been weeks since we foiled the attack. They must have carried out inquests and reviews of every detail.'

'Will they support you?'

'Again, I don't know,' I said.' There is always the old, old problem of reluctance to upset our most powerful ally. It's the same worry I have with the MoD. I'm sure they don't really believe the US allegation about Tim. What I'm afraid of is that they will agree to hold the inquiry but speak out strongly in Tim's favour – as a kind of diplomatic compromise.'

'You're right of course. If that happens, Overton's career will inevitably be damaged, even if he is cleared. Leave this with me. I'll martial as much evidence as I possibly can and then I'll contact Hartnett. Meanwhile, you must do your best to get MI6 to move into action on your behalf.'

Standish stood up. 'I'd better go to Patricia.'

He offered his hand and I shook it gratefully.

'Before I go, Sir, may I just say, once and for all, I am so sorry about Sarah.'

'I know you are and for what it's worth, I don't blame you for what happened. You were badly treated by MI6. You carried out your mission in the Middle East in an exemplary fashion. You can be proud of that.'

He withdrew his hand and half turned to Cayman.

'You can say in your article that it's been very hard for both Patricia and me. In the army, we talk quite calmly about collateral damage in an operation. But it is very hard when the collateral damage is your own daughter.'

When he was inside the house, I suggested that we go to the nearby village for a meal and a mini celebration before flying back to Weymouth.

'I didn't think it could possibly go this well,' I said, 'he has a very quiet manner, but once he decides to go after Hartnett, he won't give up easily.'

Cayman hesitated.

'Would you mind if I went on to London. I can get a taxi to Tonbridge then a train. I'd like to check in with the bureau then come back to Weymouth tomorrow.'

I smiled. 'Let me guess,' I said, 'what you're really saying is you don't want to fly in my beloved Tiger Moth again.'

Cayman smiled back. 'If you're inviting me to be frank, I would do almost anything to avoid it!'

I called her a taxi then walked back to the Tiger Moth, careful to skirt the house as I didn't want to risk Patricia seeing me again. The flight back to Portland was uneventful and I called Tim and asked him to pick me up at the farm strip. We sat in the car at the side of the runway and I briefed him on the Standish meeting. It had gone better than I could have possibly hoped, but I was careful not to be over optimistic.

'Standish is a good officer,' Tim said, 'and I'm very grateful to you and Chunk. He can only help, but it may take a lot more than one man's word. This has gone way high up.'

I could see Tim had been brooding, which was so completely unlike him. I had never seen him this shaken. In battle he was fearless, a natural leader, with a 'never give up' approach that inspired confidence in the tightest of corners. This kind of attack was far more devastating than anything we were used to and it showed, despite his cheerful expressions of gratitude.

I made sure the Tiger was safely locked in its barn-cum-hangar and asked if I could borrow Tim's car to visit Kate in Dorchester.

'I presume she's awake,' I said.

Tim managed a smile. 'Oh yes, awake and teeth bared. The hospital won't let her out yet, so Dorset may be minus a surgeon or two before the week's out.'

On the way to the hospital, I managed to buy some roses that didn't look like a last minute garage purchase. I arrived just inside visiting hours but I think I would have been let in anyway, as I was clearly a figure of intense curiosity to the nurses and support staff.

Kate was sitting up in bed, dressed in a blue hospital gown, and looking decidedly belligerent.

'Nice roses,' she said, unconvincingly, as I gave her a greeting kiss.

'They're to thank you for saving my life,' I said, 'if that doesn't sound too cheesy.'

I squeezed her hand. 'What you did was very brave. That arrow could have gone right through you.'

'That does sound cheesy,' she said lightly, 'but if you're grateful, you can do something for me.'

'What?'

'Roses are great, but what I really want is chocolate. Lots of chocolate.'

'I didn't know you were a chocoholic.'

I had never seen her eating much chocolate, except for the occasional nibble.

'Only at certain times. Sometimes at sea, when I've hit a rough patch, I dream of chocolate. Right now, I feel as though I'm becalmed in the Southern Oceans, only worse.'

'I'll go and get some,' I said. I glanced at my watch. 'If they'll let me back in.'

'I'll make sure they do,' Kate said, and her tone left no doubt she meant it.

I left the ward and managed to find a late-night convenience store that sold decent quality Swiss chocolate and bought a dozen bars. When I got back, her face softened for the first time as she unwrapped one and offered me a piece.

'I wouldn't dare deprive you,' I said.

'I know it's silly, she said, 'I'll probably only eat half a bar. But knowing it's there is comforting.'

'I'm sorry I couldn't come earlier,' I said and explained where I had been.

'Did it go well?' Kate asked.

'Very well. But Tim's still worried.'

'Has he reason to be?'

'I think we all have,' I said, 'but we will get there in the end.'

I knew it was a phrase I'd been using too much lately and it didn't do much for Kate's mood. When I tried to say more about how grateful I was for her bravery on the boat, she brushed it aside and ate some more chocolate. I asked if she was in pain and she assured me she wasn't.

'I was hoping to see Bob,' I said, 'but Leslie has sworn death on me if I go anywhere near him.'

'Don't worry about him, Kate said, 'he's doing fine. He's just down the corridor. I've seen him two or three times and I've promised Leslie we'll only talk about sailing.'

I decided to risk the big question.

'You've heard nothing from Ocean Reports, I suppose.'

Kate shook her head. 'Not a word, but Sandra's doing a great job so I'm not being missed.'

We both knew that the Games coverage wasn't what we were talking about, but I deliberately let it pass.

Superficially, she was being cheerful but in a brittle kind of way and it was clearly no time to talk about anything important. We chatted quietly until a nurse came in and told me politely that it really was time for me to leave.

'When will you be out?' I asked as I kissed her good-bye.

'They won't give me a firm date yet,' she said. 'If they try to keep me much longer, you'll be reading about hospital violence in the *Dorset Echo*.'

When I got to the car park, I checked my phones. There was nothing except a missed call notification on my regular cell.

It wasn't a number I recognised, but before I got into the car, I pressed the return call button.

'Thank you for calling back, Mr Saxon,' a polite educated voice replied.

'My name is Julian Lloyd and I have a message from Virginia Walsh. She'd like to see you tomorrow morning at 11-30. She'd like you to go to Osmington village, that's just down the coast from you.'

He gave me an address and postcode then added in the same polite voice.

'Mrs Walsh says its important you don't miss the meeting and would you kindly come alone.'

15

As I drove the four miles east down the coast to Osmington, I tried to decide how best to handle Virginia. I'd thought about it for much of the night and still wasn't sure whether to be conciliatory or threatening. Over the years, I had compiled a considerable dossier of the manoeuvring and dirty dealing she had indulged in during her struggle to rise to the top of the intelligence heap. I could exert pressure, but, thanks to UpstairsBackstairs, any moral high ground I possessed had now crumbled under my feet. For the first time ever, I felt potentially at Virginia's mercy – and that was not a comfortable place to be. Nevertheless, it was always dangerous to be too conciliatory with Virginia as exploiting weakness was her speciality.

When Lloyd had given me the address, he had said I should park in the centre of the village and take an alleyway at the end of the lane in front of the church. I followed the directions and found a very attractive detached cottage, distinguished from others in the lane by a door painted in eggshell blue, to tone with the wisteria which covered most of the front wall.

I saw Virginia straightaway. She was dressed as I had never seen her before, in a very casual summer dress patterned with cornflowers, with her hair loose around her shoulders.

She was in the kitchen garden, helping a powerfully built, athletic-looking young man to carry boxes into the side door. I went to the fence and offered to help, but she waved a refusal and told me to go inside and wait in the lounge, promising that she would not be long. The cottage was beautiful, cosy and tastefully furnished. The lounge was at the back, looking out over a pleasantly wild garden with a pond and rockery. I looked around but there was no obvious sign who the cottage belonged to. On the walls was a set of coloured prints that looked as though they had been done by a local artist and there were no personal photographs or memorabilia. I wandered around a little, but very discreetly as this time I did not want to antagonise Virginia. Looking through the windows on all sides of the cottage I could see no sign of her official Mercedes or any bodyguards. Though the young man looked fit enough, he didn't have the bodyguard look. He could be a relative or even a lover. There was no way of telling.

'You came unprotected,' I said, when Virginia appeared a few minutes later.

'Yes, I'm preparing to get used to it.'

'Why?' I asked, though I guessed the answer before she gave it.

'I'm leaving the service. Would you like a drink before lunch?'

I asked for a fruit juice and tried to hide my concern. I knew she was treating it deliberately casually as a kind of teasing. She knew full well that the implications for me were very serious.

'What made you decide?' I asked.

She continued to pour herself a drink without looking directly at me.

'A number of things. I'm divorcing my husband so it seemed a good time to make a double break.'

'Can I ask what happened with your husband?'

Virginia came over and motioned me to sit on the sofa while she sat in an armchair opposite.

'He's been planning a rather nasty little coup,' she began, 'for some time as a matter of fact. At the moment, he is living in Ecuador with some kind of mail-order bride or something. He has been very carefully siphoning off money and putting it in out-of-the-way places. He was also planning to sell the St John's Wood house out from under me. He had in mind to leave me destitute and play house with his bimbo. So much for Accountants for the Risen Christ!'

Her husband had always made a great show of his Christianity and this was one of several evangelical groups in which he was supposedly active.

'From the way you said that, I gather he didn't succeed.'

'No, fortunately he's not a brave man. He wasn't hard to scare. I took a leaf out of your book. I told him I couldn't do anything about getting the money back because I couldn't match his financial expertise, but I did have other skills.'

She paused but I said, 'please go on, I'm fascinated'

'I told him if he went ahead with his plan, he would never be at ease ever again, even in Ecuador, in fact especially in Ecuador. I reminded him that I had access to people who would do things to his body that he couldn't even imagine in his worst nightmares. I didn't have to spell out the details. We agreed on a very satisfactory financial settlement and the money miraculously reappeared in my bank account.'

'So what you plan to do? Are you considering politics?'

Virginia laughed. 'No not politics, embroidery!'

She saw my look and added, 'don't pretend you haven't seen my work. I know you searched the house when you came to St John's Wood.'

'It was very beautiful. I was impressed.'

'I hope enough people think so. I'm planning to go into business. I shall start in a small way at first, but I hope it will grow. Shall we have lunch?'

By now, I was seriously concerned. This kind of complete break from MI6 was really bad news. I had never enjoyed dealing with Virginia but I had learned how to do it. There were too many unknowns already. This was one too many.

'Shall I call the young man?' I asked, as she put the finishing touches to setting the table.

'No, this is a working lunch.'

She didn't elaborate but the implication was clear. The young man was strictly for pleasure. Presumably he went with the new embroidery-oriented Virginia. The world was indeed full of surprises.

The first course was shrimp salad and as we sat down, she said, 'the other reason I decided to leave was that I've finally had enough. Struggling to become Queen of the Labyrinth, as you all call it, is more tiring than you might think. I could well make it to the top, but I am fifty-two and I decided it was time to make a break while I still have some energy left.'

She gave me a mischievous smile. 'I can see I've finally managed to get to you. You're wondering what all this means for you - whether I'm going to help you.'

'Yes, obviously I'm concerned.'

'Well, as it happens, you needn't be. I am going to help you. You've been treated very badly in the past and I owe you an apology.'

Then with a sudden flash of the old Virginia she added, 'but understand this: the apology is strictly personal not professional. As a human being I'm sorry about what has happened to you. Professionally, I have no regrets. I believe I did the right thing after Rome. You may disagree, but I'm afraid that can't be helped. You wanted us to go to war with Washington on your behalf, but they were bigger concerns at the time that were not linked to your problems.'

She smiled suddenly and I think, for the first time in all my experience of her, it was a genuine one.

'But I am sorry and I'm actually in a position to put things right, and I don't mean just what happened in Rome, I also mean what's happening now.'

I could see she was still teasing me as she made me wait until she had served the next course before continuing.

'We've been watching you flounder in the face of this online onslaught. Your beloved network is completely at sea and so are you. It's been a most interesting exercise watching you struggle, not knowing how to respond. Fortunately, we have a brand-new department dealing with this online world. It concerns itself with cyber security, hacking, online radicalisation, trolling, the dark web, abuse of social media and a whole lot more. As you've discovered to your cost, this new kind of warfare can be as damaging as terrorism.'

'So you know what Ray Vossler was up to. There was no sting operation. The attack was intended to discredit Teheran.'

'Of course. But as you've discovered, fighting back isn't completely straightforward. For example, you believe that this attack on you is being run by Maxine Herald, don't you?'

'Isn't it?'

'No, it's being masterminded by a man called Carlos Alvarez. He's a Hispanic-American under contract to the Vosslers and has been parachuted into Maxine Herald's organisation. His background is half Hollywood, half Silicon Valley. His speciality is manipulating social media. He's worked for a number of corporations, planting lies, creating false images, generally distorting reality to keep unpleasant truths hidden. He's also worked on political campaigns in the US and Eastern Europe.'

'How do you know all this?'

'Luckily for you, my attempts to become Queen of the Labyrinth have involved cultivating good relations with MI5. They've had a man inside Maxine Herald's organisation for some time, long before Alvarez arrived, in fact. Their man is quite senior actually and good at his job. In fact, he's been helping Alvarez plan your downfall. We've had to be careful about that. We don't want anyone accusing him of being an agent provocateur.'

Through the window, I could see the young man pottering about in the garden, weeding and watering plants, providing a completely surreal background to the conversation.

'Is Alvarez behind UpstairsBackstairs?' I asked.

'No, U-B is just the platform he's chosen to launch the ideas he wants the social media to pick up on. We could close UpstairsBackstairs down but we prefer not to. They would only choose a platform that is harder to deal with, one in China or Russia or North Korea.'

'Isn't that where UpstairsBackstairs is based?'

'No, it's run from a farmhouse near Dublin by some graduates who think it's fun to take the piss out of the mainstream media.'

Before I could comment, Virginia got up from the table, went over to a desk in the corner and brought back a thick folder.

'I'm going to give you three presents to mark my retirement,' she said. 'The first is this dossier. It contains complete documentation on Ray Vossler's activities in Iraq, Jordan, Lebanon and Syria. You'll recognise a lot of it because most of it is your work. You did an excellent job and we've also included everything else we have on Vossler from other sources. He really is a thoroughly slimy, corrupt and dangerous individual.'

She tapped the file. 'There's enough here to make him squirm for the next decade and, with a bit of luck, sink him altogether. The second part of the dossier contains everything the MI5 mole has documented about the campaign against you and your so-called network, seen from the inside of Maxine Herald's organisation. It contains detailed accounts of the meetings to orchestrate the lies that have been told about you on UpstairsBackstairs.'

She grinned. 'And as a small bonus I've included some information from the Met about charges that they hope will be laid soon against Maxine Herald for domestic slavery. It seems she's been ruthlessly exploiting a couple of Saudi girls who run her house in Belgravia. The Met almost has enough proof to charge her, but anyway, that needn't stop the information being published as we choose.'

'There's really not much I can say,' I said.

'Then don't say anything. I'm sure you did enough talking when you saw General Standish yesterday. Yes, we have been keeping an eye on you. Seeing your former father-in-law was quite something. It can't have been an easy meeting.'

'It wasn't.'

'You went on Tim Overton's behalf, of course.'

'Yes.'

'Did he agree to help?'

'Yes.'

'Good! We can help there too. I presume you wanted Standish to see General Hartnett?'

'Yes.'

'He will be a good intermediary and I will make sure he receives full details of the plan that Alvarez concocted to discredit Overton. There should be more than enough to convince Hartnett that he is backing the wrong horse.'

I sat looking across at Virginia utterly speechless. It was a cliché but I genuinely didn't know what to say. Virginia saw my discomfort and was clearly enjoying it.

'Now for my second present,' she said, 'having all this information is all very well but nobody in your network really has the skills to exploit it.' Virginia got up and went to the window and signalled to the young man in the garden.

'I'm sure you've been fantasising about my young lover, all ready to pleasure me when you go back to your boat.' She smiled. 'Don't I wish, but that's not what this is about.'

The young man came in and Virginia made the introductions.

'This is Robert Grayling, the Deputy Head of our Cyber Security Section. I'm going to loan him to you for a couple of weeks. The boxes you saw us bringing in contain computer equipment. This is going to be his base for a while and his task is to put things right for you. We have to admit that Alvarez has done a damn good job and there's a great deal to put right. But don't worry, Robert has been closely monitoring all the attacks on you and the network. Some of it can be sorted out with a few discreet official phone calls, but most of it will need a media campaign which Robert will run.'

'I'm sure we'll get on just fine,' Grayling said. 'And don't worry, I'll liaise with you, so you won't get any more unpleasant surprises.'

I thanked him and turned back to Virginia. 'I've had some surprises in my life,' I said, 'but this has to rate, without question, at number one.'

'I'm glad,' she said, 'I put a lot of thought into planning it.'

'Assuming all goes well, can I ask about my own future afterwards.'

Virginia's tone was still friendly but suddenly business-like again.

'That's one thing I can't help you with,' she said, 'I'll have to leave that to the Chief. If you do come back in, the best job for you would be Head of Middle East Operations but that's not going to happen. There's a new man in there and he is doing a good job. But don't despair, they may well find something decent for you in due time.'

She said it in a tone that made clear she wasn't expecting an answer or an argument. Instead she went over to the desk again and this time she brought back a large brown package.

'This is your third present,' she said, 'do unwrap it!'

I pulled open the paper and inside found a large cushion. It was exquisitely embroidered with the motif of a classical labyrinth. At the centre was a smiling female face with a crown perched jauntily on her head.

16

I came back to Weymouth in a euphoric mood but I was careful not to be too enthusiastic when I briefed the team. I had known Virginia for many years and though I was confident her change of heart was real, the others didn't know her well enough to make that judgement and were bound to be sceptical. When I had finished my account of the Osmington meeting, Birdy said, 'it sounds good but the transformation from bitch from hell to warm-hearted embroiderer is going to take a bit of getting used to.' It was the reaction I'd expected and I'd already decided my next move.

'If you're happy to do it, Jay,' I said, 'I'd like you to go to Osmington to meet Grayling. We could use a second opinion. He's already said he wants to liaise with us and you're the obvious one to do it.'

Everyone liked the idea and I had guessed right. When Jay came back three hours later, it was his report, rather than mine, that convinced everyone we were about to turn a corner.

Tim, Birdy, Lottery, Chunk and I assembled again on board the *Jessica* and we saw immediately that Jay had been impressed.

'That Grayling is something else,' he said.

'But does he know what he's about?' Birdy asked.

Jay laughed. 'Judge for yourself. I started out by explaining our private communications network and told him I had brought a handset so I could link him in. Do you know what he said?'

'No, what?'

'The devious bastard said, 'Oh I've been on your network since you set it up.' Would you credit it? Six have been listening to every single bloody word we've been saying.'

'Jesus,' Tim said, 'that is impressive – and scary.'

'Grayling is hard at work already,' Jay went on, 'take a look at ARRSE.' The Army Rumour Service, ARRSE was the unofficial army website that soldiers used to communicate with each other. We logged in and we saw that Grayling had anonymously initiated a forum of support for Tim which was already getting a huge response. There was warm praise for him from scores of soldiers and the number was rising minute by minute. 'A bit embarrassing,' Tim said, but couldn't hide his satisfaction.

ARRSE was strictly unofficial, but the MoD couldn't possibly ignore a forum like that.

'And it gets better, much better,' Jay said. 'The MI6 Chief, Sir Jeremy Peacock, has already contacted Standish and asked him to fly to Washington at Six's expense to brief Hartnett face to face. Grayling showed me the material General Standish will be taking with him and I think you really can start to relax a bit now, Tim.'

For the first time since the cowardice allegation had surfaced, a real smile came to Tim's face. He didn't need to say anything. We all knew that we had finally started to win.

We were about to break up, but Jay hadn't finished.

'I have to admire the guy,' Jay said, 'even though he's been hacking into my network. With Virginia's approval, he's arranged for Peacock to hold a private briefing for all the editors and senior people in the main news organisations. He's going to tell them the whole story about Maxine Herald and Alvarez and the campaign they've been running to discredit you lot, as well as claiming Ray Vossler's attack on London was a sting operation. Peacock will make it absolutely clear that whatever MI6 says in the next few days will have his full authority behind it. Then, after the mainstream media have started to run the story, Grayling's going to set social media alight with stuff that will have the whole Vossler gang screaming blue murder.'

Finally, I got the collective sigh of relief I had been hoping for. Even Chunk, whose family troubles were not connected, acknowledged that restoring the network's credibility could only help him. Birdy was also more confident that his CO would be happier, while Tim reported that Rachel was well on the way to sorting out her own problems.

'And my problems are also coming good,' Lottery said, triumphantly. 'My girlfriend has agreed to give me another chance. She's coming back to Weymouth.'

'Which is my cue to head for Dorchester,' I said, 'it's nearly visiting hours. I have to tell Kate the good news.'

I didn't want to spoil the mood on board the *Jessica* but I knew that none of this was necessarily going to solve Kate's problem with Ocean Reports or, for that matter, Marie's chances of establishing her new law practice. She had returned to London yet again, this time to meet the French lawyer she hoped to team up with, as well as their English associates. A lot was riding on the meeting, but she had not been optimistic it would go well. There was nothing I could do to help Marie for the moment but I thought the Grayling news would at least cheer Kate up a bit. Still, I knew a lot more had to be done and before I had even set off for the hospital, her problem got a great deal bigger.

UpstairsBackstairs launched a story with the headline:

Yachtie Kate hospitalised to deal with aftermath of abortion.

The story was written in a tone of phoney sympathy for 'Poor Kate' whose relationship with 'failed spook John Saxon' was 'continuing to cause her nothing but grief.'

When I got to the hospital, I was expecting her to be furious, but it was worse than that, she was quiet and depressed.

When I asked if her shoulder was causing her much pain, she replied, 'don't you mean my lost baby,' adding gloomily, 'sorry, I didn't mean that. I'm doing my best to stay positive but a girl can only take so much.'

Kate said the hospital was mad as hell and they were going to arrange for an examination by a senior gynaecologist who would issue a formal statement saying she had never been pregnant and that there had been no abortion.

'It probably won't do much good,' she said, 'UpstairsBackstairs will probably run a story headed, **Hospital cover-up to save yachtie Kate.**'

'The statement has to help with Ocean Reports,' I said.

Kate grunted. 'Something had better. You haven't heard the latest. I've had an email from the editor saying he was sorry about my difficulties but my services would definitely not be needed for the Paralympics and asking whether 'in the circumstances' we could shorten the charter of the *Jurassic Star.*'

'Is the Publisher behind this?'

'No idea,' Kate said, 'the editor doesn't need his authority. He's in charge of the coverage of the Games.'

I told her about Grayling but it did nothing to cheer her up. She listened then said quietly, 'John, will you come with me to Norfolk?'

'Yes of course,' I said, 'but why Norfolk?'

'I need to get away from all this. I just want to hide somewhere until it all settles down. I've spoken to Bob and he's found us a boat. You and I need some time together. We have a lot to talk about.'

I had no idea what she meant by 'having a lot to talk about.' I hoped it was good news but this wasn't the moment to try to probe any deeper.

'When are they going to let you out?' I asked.

'Tomorrow afternoon. They're determined to get me out in time for the end of the Games and all the celebrations and parties, as if that's what I wanted. I never thought you'd hear me say this, but I don't want to be among sailors at the moment.'

'We've sort of guessed that,' I said, 'Birdy is going to organise a quiet party somewhere, probably on board the *Nova Scotia*.'

'Do I have to go?'

'Of course not, but it would be nice if we went for a while. We can always use your shoulder as an excuse and slip away early.'

'If we must,' Kate said. 'I'm surprised Bouncer's family will let us near their beautiful boat, after we set fire to it.'

'Seems they're not bothered at all. The brother, Davie, plans to use the insurance money to make all kinds of improvements.'

'Then straight to Norfolk afterwards, is that okay?'

'Can you manage the Tiger with that shoulder?' I asked.

'Just try and stop me,' she said. It was a flash of the old Kate and a good note to end on. I asked if I should see Bob but Kate said, 'absolutely not. Don't go near him or Leslie will kill you. I'll tell him about Grayling.'

On the way back to Weymouth, I decided I would go to see Grayling the next morning to ask him whether he could do more for Kate. It was obvious that MI6's priority was setting the record straight about Vossler's attack. Fortunately that involved dealing with the network's credibility, especially mine and Tim's, but Kate risked getting lost in the shuffle.

Late that night, Marie came back from London and, if anything, she was more depressed than Kate.

'Everyone is being very nice,' she said, 'but it's going to be a hell of a struggle setting up my new practice. I don't honestly think it's ever going to happen.'

I told her what had happened at the meeting with Virginia. Her reaction was very much like Kate's. She was pleased for us, but her own problems were uppermost. I said I was hoping to see Grayling the next morning and, on an impulse, I suggested she come with me.

She agreed but was still fairly noncommittal. 'It might help,' she said, 'and anything that gets me away from that boat can't be bad.'

I phoned Grayling to arrange a meeting for the next morning and we drove to Osmington in Birdy's car. When we arrived, Grayling was bright with enthusiasm.

'I like your *New York Times* woman, Sheila Cayman,' he said enthusiastically, 'she's being very cooperative.'

'In what way?' I asked. 'I haven't spoken to her since she left for London.'

'I've invited Cayman to the Chief's briefing,' Grayling said, 'and we've made a deal. She's agreed not to publish anything until we launch our main campaign – I didn't want the Brits to feel they were playing catch-up with the Americans - in return, I'm going to give her a good chunk of extra material. Also, the ARRSE campaign is going really well and you're going to like this, there's been a meeting with Heather Fenton.'

I asked what kind of meeting and Grayling laughed.

'We sent Jean Bullock. You won't know her. She's a recent recruit. Not very experienced yet but born devious. She told Fenton that MI6 was anxious to avoid a scandal and she had come for a little private chat. Bullock said you'd be suing her for slander and we would be paying your legal expenses, as MI6 felt it had a duty of care towards you.'

'I like that bit,' I said.

'Yes, well, Bullock told Fenton she assumed Vossler would be paying her costs and with both sides well-funded, the trial could be lengthy, what with having to bring witnesses from Jordan and so on. Bullock said that with such a high-profile case, the costs would probably start at around £100,000 for each side and could end up being double that. Bullock said she thought Fenton might be going to have a heart attack, so she eased up a bit and said MI6 was anxious to avoid a court case and would Fenton consider talking to Vossler about reaching an out of court settlement.

'No-one is going to sue of course, but we've given Fenton a few nightmares and we won't be hearing much from her when we start demolishing all her tosh.

'Now,' he said, 'what did you want to talk about?'

I told him that everyone was delighted with his efforts and I passed on Tim's special thanks. But, I said, two careers were still in serious jeopardy – Kate's and Marie's.

'Yes, I have given that some thought,' Grayling said. He smiled apologetically at Marie. 'If you don't mind, I'll start with Kate, as her problem is a bit easier. I've been back in touch with our man inside Maxine Herald's organisation. He's promised to give me any extra detail he can about how they worked up the phoney pregnancy and abortion story. Combined with a reputable medical denial, that should go a long way towards putting things right. I thought we might start with some articles planted in key sailing magazines. I considered asking Sandra Snow to help, but I think she's too close to you all. Anyway, it might take a little time, but I'm sure we'll get there.'

He turned to Marie, 'I have to admit though that your problem is trickier.'

'Why is that?' I interrupted.

'To be blunt,' Grayling said, 'we have much less to work with. The photo at the Auberge des Fleurs – it was taken by a drone by the way – was pretty damning.'

'Nothing whatever happened between us,' I said. I went on to explain the background, about our past history at the Auberge, why we were sharing a room, about the teasing and the jokes about me not being French, all of it in fun. Grayling listened carefully and made notes but I could feel myself floundering and eventually it was Marie who put a stop to it.

With a rueful smile, she said, 'John, if I were your lawyer, I wouldn't put you anywhere near a witness stand. Any half-decent barrister would tear you to shreds – and me with you!'

'I'm glad you see the difficulty,' Grayling said, 'that's always the trouble with sex. The minute you start talking about it, distortions kick in. Also,' he hesitated, clearly not wanting to offend Marie, 'there is the inescapable fact: in Weymouth you do seem to be a triangle. As I understand it, forgive me, we have been listening to a lot of your chit-chat, Marie even hates boats and there wasn't any obvious reason for her to come to Weymouth, except to see you.'

'She was the one who tipped us off about Maxine Herald in the first place,' I objected, 'she came to warn us.'

'You could argue she could have done that by phone,' Grayling said, 'but I do sympathise, I really do, and I promise I'll do everything I possibly can.'

I could see there was nothing more to be said, so I thanked him, refused his offer of coffee, and we went out into the village. As we passed the church, Marie pointed to the graveyard. 'That looks like a nice shady spot for a walk,' she said.

We strolled along the paths through the overgrown but still beautiful, flower-strewn headstones, and Marie kept a discreet distance from me, careful to give no hint of intimacy.

'Grayling is quite right, I do realise that,' she said.

'He's certainly right about sex becoming distorted once you try to explain it. It's much better done than talked about.'

'He's right about Weymouth too.'

I nodded. 'Yes, it does look compromising.'

I tried to lighten the mood. 'It's a pity he can't plant some articles in some key law journals as well as the sailing magazines.'

'That would be fun,' Marie said. 'The trouble is you're supposed to tell the truth in law journals and, I may as well admit it, the truth is I was trying to win you back.'

'Teasing me into bed to see if I'm committed to Kate hardly qualifies as trying to win me back.'

Marie smiled. 'Oh, John, it was much more than that. I liked John Cartwright well enough. He was a lot of fun, but I am more than a bit in love with John Saxon.'

I was so startled I didn't know what to say, but before I could speak she had taken my hand and guided me to a clump of trees in the corner of the graveyard.

'Don't worry,' she said, 'it's over. I have given up. I know when I'm beaten. Whatever I feel for you, I'm not sure I could have done what Kate did on the boat. She could easily have been killed.'

'I think that was instinct as much as love,' I said.

Marie's answer was almost sharp. 'Don't be foolish, John, you have to love someone a lot to throw down your life. I'd like to think I'd have done the same, but we'll never know.'

She put her arm round me. 'I'm going back to London then on to Paris and I want a farewell kiss, a proper one.' She looked around. 'No drones, no paparazzi, just us.'

The kiss was long, tender and passionate and I could feel her warmth through my whole body.

When I tried to speak afterwards, she put a finger over my lips and on the drive back, she did nothing to try to prolong the moment. She refused to talk about anything except the scenery and the Olympic Games and how much she had enjoyed meeting the members of the network.

When we reached Weymouth she asked to be dropped at the station.

'What about your things?' I said.

'Rachel is bringing them later. Please say my good-byes to everyone, especially Kate.' She smiled. 'I'm sure she won't miss me.'

I was still so stunned, all I could think of to say was, 'I'll make sure Grayling does his best for you.'

'I know you will,' Marie said, as she walked away from the car, 'you're that kind of man,' and a moment later she was gone.

17

The next day it became all-out war, and this time it looked like being our kind of battleground.

I got a call from Virginia. She was trying to sound professional but she was distraught and agitated.

'Ray Vossler has found out what we're doing. He's already left London and sworn to wipe you out, once and for all.'

'Tell me exactly what happened,' I said, 'and we'll deal with it.'

'As far as we can reconstruct it,' Virginia continued, gaining control of her voice, 'the Vosslers got wind of the briefing the Chief is giving to editors and they also know about Grayling. Immediately, Ivan and Mark started talking about going back to the States.'

'Leaving little brother Ray to swing in the wind?'

'Yes. There was a crisis meeting in their hotel suite and that was when Ray went crazy.

'Our informant said he started screaming and ranting. In fact he completely lost it. He swore he'd never go back to prison and said he'd get his revenge on you, whatever the cost. Then he vanished and we've lost track of him.'

'Wonderful,' I said, 'what is anyone doing about it?'

'There's a general alert out for him, of course. He could still get out of the country, although he's surrendered his passport as part of his bail conditions, but we have to assume he's heading for Weymouth.

'I've spoken to Inspector Frampton and to his Chief Constable. Frampton will be given whatever extra resources he feels he needs. I'm taking Grayling out of Dorset. He'll carry on with the campaign from London.'

Just for a moment, Virginia's tone softened.

'I'm sorry about this, John. Everything was going so well. Do watch your back.'

Frampton called minutes later and said he had arranged a police guard for Kate at the hospital.

'I'm sending two police cars to the Marina,' he said. 'I want to see you all as soon as possible. I need to know everything about this Ray Vossler. Your Mrs Walsh says he could be extremely dangerous.'

I decided to take no chances with Kate. Chunk was already on his way to the hospital to say good-bye, as had been summoned to the Ministry of Defence. He agreed to check on what security Frampton had arranged.

Two police cars arrived. The first took Tim, Rachel and Birdy. Lottery, Jay and I followed and we were taken to a modern, glass and stainless steel building that Weymouth police shared with the Fire and Rescue Service. We were guided to a conference room and found Frampton with two uniformed sergeants from the Olympic Games security team – one from Devon and one from Surrey. They didn't look happy and I guessed that they were winding down and had been looking forward to the final night of celebrations before going back to their own forces.

Frampton made the introductions and the two sergeants immediately focused their attention on Rachel. The Devon sergeant, Al Phillips, gave no sign of knowing anything about her but was clearly intrigued that she outranked them all. The second officer, Phil King, had obviously seen the UpstairsBackstairs stories. For a brief moment, his eyes fell on her breasts then he found himself caught in Rachel's steely gaze and he quickly looked down at the table. Hazel, the Police Community Support Officer who had accompanied us to the press conference, came to join us and gave Tim and Lottery a friendly smile. If this was the extra support Virginia had promised, I thought, it was not looking good.

Frampton turned to Rachel. 'I presume it's alright with you, Ma'am, if I conduct the briefing? It was the first time that Frampton had addressed her formally and Rachel responded accordingly.

'Of course, Inspector,' she said. 'Please carry on.'

In order to flag Rachel's credentials to the visiting sergeants, Frampton said politely, 'I believe you've met Vossler yourself, Ma'am, while you were directing the training of police forces in Iraq.'

'I did,' Rachel said. 'All of us, except Jay, have met him at some point in our careers, but John and Tim know him best.

'Good,' Frampton said. 'I've told our colleagues what the situation is. They will call on more of their men, as the situation develops. What I need from you all now is the fullest possible picture of the man.'

I took my cue and stood up.

'Ray Vossler is about to stand trial for organising a bio-terrorist attack on London,' I said. 'He has strong connections with the US intelligence community, despite being first and foremost a financial crook specialising in international money-laundering.'

'You mean the CIA,' Sergeant Phillips interrupted.

'Vossler has worked for the CIA in the past,' I said, 'but he's currently tied in with a fringe intelligence group with loose affiliation to the US Department of Defense.'

Neither Phillips nor King registered much interest.

Frampton by contrast was quick with the pertinent question.

'Exactly how dangerous is Ray Vossler as an individual?'

'His main skill is organising operations,' I said, 'but he can definitely be dangerous and ruthless.'

Phillips' face remained blank.

I spoke directly to Frampton.

'Virginia Walsh says Vossler is so angry and irrational, there's no telling what he might do.'

'Are we sure the spooks aren't getting excited over nothing,' Phillips said.

I glanced at Lottery who was watching the Sergeant closely and, I guessed, itching to punch him.

Sergeant King appeared to be staring out of the picture window across the rooftops beyond. We were getting nowhere. Frampton was obviously annoyed but was not willing to reprimand either of them in front of us. Instead he focused on questioning me.

'Does Vossler have any military skills?' he asked.

'Yes, he does.'

'Is he any good?'

'No, that's where the danger lies.'

Phillips sighed and at this point Tim intervened.

'Let me explain exactly what John means,' he said.

'Ray Vossler has two brothers, Ivan and Mark. They're both military types. Ivan quarterbacked the West Point football team and served in the infantry. Mark was airborne. They both have good service records and Ray has a massive chip on his shoulder about them. He feels completely overshadowed.

'To try to prove he isn't just a money man, he persuaded the CIA to let him go to The Farm, that's the CIA training facility at Camp Peary, Virginia, where he did the short training course.'

'Did he fail?' Frampton asked.

'No, he did quite well. He prepared in advance and got himself physically fit. He more or less coped with the rough stuff and he was brilliant at the theory. But I've been to Peary and I've talked to his instructor and his final report was damning.'

'Why?'

'The bottom line was that he lacked self-control and was 'liable to panic' in any tight corner.'

Tim paused. 'And believe me, Inspector, I've trained a lot of men and there's nothing more dangerous than someone who loses it when the going gets tough.'

'Yes, I see the problem,' Frampton said. 'Anything else?'

'He has access to unlimited funds. He can get hold of anything he needs,' I said.'

'You mean weapons?'

'Possibly, but he can certainly recruit help.

'He'll probably use Sanders and Waugh at least,' Tim said.

'Surely they won't get involved,' Frampton said, 'they're already facing criminal damage charges.'

'Vossler has a very strong hold over them,' Tim said, 'they'll do anything he asks, regardless.'

'Right then,' Frampton said, 'Sergeant Phillips, do you know who these men are?'

'No, Sir.

'Then find out, and arrest them.'

'On what charge?'

'Suspicion of making false declarations to the police, or whatever occurs to you. Just bring them in, Understood?'

'Sergeant King,' Frampton said, without waiting for an answer from Phillips.

'Sir.'

'I want you to round up twelve men from the Olympic security team and report with them to the marina.'

'But Sir, our assignment ends tonight,' King objected.

Frampton's reply was curt. 'No, it doesn't. If you want to take it up with your Super, have him call me and I'll make sure you get the necessary authority.'

When they had left, Hazel rolled her eyes.

'You can't blame them,' Frampton said. 'They were all set to join in tonight's partying, then go home. Go after Phillips, Hazel, and help him dig out everything we have on Sanders and Waugh.'

When she had left, Frampton said, 'we need a frank word and, Chief Inspector Hunter, I'd be grateful if you could close your ears for a moment.'

Rachel smiled. 'Don't worry, Inspector, I know what you're going to say and I won't drop you in it.'

The relief showed clearly on Frampton's face.

'You can see my problem,' he said. 'It's not going to be easy to get the Olympic guys worked up about Vossler and I'm going to need your help. You know him and you have the military skills we may need. But I've said it before and I mean it: I am not going to allow a private war between you lot and whatever gang Vossler manages to recruit. Can I count on you to help on those terms?'

I didn't need to consult the others. 'Yes, you can, Inspector, we will do everything we can to help you, and don't worry, we won't destroy your career.'

I turned to the group.

'There's one thing none of us must forget. We don't want Vossler hurt, and we especially don't want him killed, even by accident.'

Frampton looked surprised.

'Absolutely, but why is that important to you?'

'We want Vossler in one piece to go to trial,' I said. 'We don't want a martyr who can be exploited by UpstairsBackstairs. We're about to start winning on the social media front. We can't risk anything that could mess that up.'

'Good,' Frampton said, 'now, what about tonight? Where did you plan to be?'

'We're having a private party on board the *Nova Scotia*,' Birdy said. 'Kate didn't want to get involved with any of the sailing get-togethers. She's feeling a bit raw at the moment.'

'That won't do,' Frampton said, 'the *Nova Scotia* is far too conspicuous. We can't keep you safe on the outer harbour. There'll be thousands of people all around. There's going to be a huge party on the beach and every pub on the harbour will be heaving.'

He thought for a moment.

'You'd better come to my place.'

No-one said anything but Frampton saw our faces.

He smiled. 'Don't look so miserable. We are having a party. My Missus, Kath, will make you very welcome. It'll be mostly locals, with a few police. Our house is up on Portland, well out of the way and easy to secure.'

Frampton checked his watch.

'The party won't start till latish, but it's best you all go up there as soon as possible. I'll fix it with Kath.'

My cell vibrated and I read a text from Chunk. 'Security at hospital token. Can stay with Kate for next hour but then must go to London.'

I showed it to Birdy and he agreed to relieve Chunk.

I texted a reply, saying Birdy was on his way and asking when Kate was being released.

'Not sure, yet. Waiting for results of tests,' was the answer.

I asked Frampton if he had a police car free to bring Kate from Dorchester.

'Yes, of course, and I'll have Birdy driven up there so his car won't get left at the hospital.'

He made a call to summon a car.

'Next,' he said, when Birdy had gone, 'what about your two boats? They'll probably be the first place Vossler will make for.'

Lottery groaned. 'Does that mean I'm going to be on stag at the marina instead of going to the party? Clara will never speak to me again.'

'Definitely not,' Frampton said. 'I want all of you at my place. There will be enough police to guard the boats. I'll keep you in touch with anything that happens down there.'

'I think I can help with that,' Jay said.

Frampton looked sceptical. 'Not the drone again?'

'No. If you can get the marina manager to agree, I can arrange for their CCTV to be fed to my laptop, and we can keep an eye on everything from the party.'

From then on, all the preparations went smoothly – except for getting Kate out of hospital. Birdy relieved Chunk but there was a long wait before anyone came to begin Kate's release procedure. When Birdy tried to speed things up, he was told the Consultant had been called to an emergency but had sent word that Kate was not to be allowed to leave until there had been a final examination. According to Birdy, Kate had exploded in fury when she discovered that the final examination consisted of fitting a special sling which could not easily be removed.

'It's bloody enormous,' Kate growled, when I called to ask how she was. 'When I complained, the Consultant said she knew I'd take a normal one off the minute I got home! She was right, of course,' Kate added grudgingly, 'but it's a bloody nuisance.'

Birdy had taken a dress to the hospital so that Kate could go direct to the Framptons. She didn't want to be bothered with dresses or parties and it wouldn't fit anyway because of the sling. Finally, Rachel took another dress to the hospital and helped her get into it. While the fitting was going on, Birdy called me and said, 'talk about timing. Just as we'd got Kate calmed down a bit, she got a call from her mate at Ocean Reports telling her about the rise and rise of Sandra Snow.'

Apparently Sandra had been given a contract as Ocean Reports' permanent British Correspondent. 'It's not as though Kate wants to be a yachting journalist,' Birdy said, 'but she wasn't happy. She grunted that she was pleased for her, but when Sandra phoned her mobile, presumably to tell her the news, she wouldn't take the call. Then she switched the phone off altogether. You'd better call me if you need to talk to her.'

While this was going on, Jay had arranged for the marina's CCTV to be fed to his private secure website, and Tim, Lottery and I had scouted Frampton's house.

Frampton's wife Kath, a cheerful, homely woman in her thirties, didn't seem at all put out when her husband told her about the 'special arrangements' he would have to make for the party.

'Just keep out of my kitchen, if you wouldn't mind,' she said, 'I've got a lot of stuff still to do.'

18

The Frampton home was a surprise. It was a large stone structure perched high on the cliffs close to the Verne Prison. The house was surrounded mainly by modern bungalows, but it turned out that Framptons had lived on Portland even longer that Bouncer's Lano family and the house had been built by one of the inspector's distant forebears.

Its most striking feature was a large terrace with views across the whole of Weymouth Bay, stretching from Chesil Beach to beyond Osmington. The panorama took in the Sailing Academy, the port of Weymouth and what Frampton referred to as our 'bucket-and-spade beach', a great curve of sand which was to be the centre of the Games' closing celebrations.

Our focus though was strictly military – was the terrace a potential target? Fortunately, the ground sloped away steeply on three sides and there was only one section that might conceivably be an easy target for a sniper.

It seemed very unlikely that Vossler's attack, if it came, would be carried out that way but Frampton insisted on roping off that section with a sign saying, 'Please keep off: new planting.'

Jay was given space in a small downstairs closet to set up his laptop and monitor the marina. He began getting clear pictures straightaway and we could see Sergeant King deploying men at points along the quay and on board boats moored close to the *Jurassic Star* and the *Jessica*.

'Camera's too far away to be sure,' Lottery said, with a grin, 'but I'll bet he's not got a smiley face.'

Private parties were beginning on board the luxury cruisers and yachts moored around the marina. When we went back out onto the terrace we could hear, faintly from across the bay, music from the beach celebrations which were building up around the two screens that had been used to transmit images of the sailing. Thousands of people were gathering to say a rousing farewell to the Olympic sailors, with a parade, music, dancing and fireworks.

Frampton had put Sergeant Phillips in charge of securing the perimeter of the house. He still looked aggrieved, but Frampton had called his superintendent and Phillips had been told, in no uncertain terms, that this new assignment had to be taken seriously.

As an extra precaution, Tim and I went with him and Frampton to check the vehicles parked in the vicinity. Frampton recognised almost all of them as belonging to neighbours. He took the registration numbers of those he didn't know and called them into the station. The report came back that they were all registered to locals and none of the owners had a criminal record, apart from the odd parking ticket and one speeding offence. Phillips adjusted the cordon he had placed round the area to make it less obtrusive and we agreed also that the security operation would kept secret. The guests, even the off-duty policemen, were not to be told what was going on, unless it became absolutely necessary.

The only entrance to the grounds of the house was on the opposite side to the terrace, which made security much easier. Frampton had arranged with one his neighbours to borrow a field for parking so the guests would all be entering the grounds on foot. To avoid having to create an obvious checkpoint, Frampton asked his sister, Charlotte, to welcome everyone at the gate. She knew all the guests and two policemen were stationed discreetly nearby to block any strangers.

By the time Birdy and Rachel brought Kate, a good number of guests had arrived and the party was well underway.

Kate gave me a smile, but I could tell this was a night she just wanted to get through as quickly as possible. I explained the security arrangements and asked her not to mention Vossler to any of the guests.

She listened, but her first question was 'where is Marie? Birdy said she'd gone.'

'She had to go and see her law associates,' I said.

'Pity,' Kate said. 'I wish she'd stayed.'

'By the time Grayling has done his work, I don't think you have to worry too much about the love triangle nonsense,' I said, 'but I do wish we could have done more to help Marie. I have a feeling she may come out of this the worst of any of us.'

Kate's face tightened.

'Worse than me?'

'I touched her good arm. 'I'm sure you'll be OK,' I said, 'even if Ocean Reports doesn't come through, you'll find other sponsors.'

154

Over her shoulder, I could see more guests coming onto the terrace and, again with wonderful timing, one of them was Sandra Snow.

She headed straight over to us, her face beaming.

'I've been trying to reach you all afternoon,' she said, 'I've got some wonderful news,'

'Yes, I've heard,' Kate said stiffly. 'Congratulations, I'm sure you'll do a wonderful job.'

'No, I don't mean the job, though that is amazing,' Sandra said, 'it's your funding. It's being restored. Ocean Reports are going to back your expedition.'

Kate stared, unsure exactly what she was hearing.

'What? How do you know?'

'The publisher told me himself. Hasn't he called you? He said he was going to.'

'My cell has been switched off.'

'Yes, I tried you several times. Anyway it's definite. I've just had the weirdest job interview you can imagine. I was supposed to do a kind of selection board by Skype, with the editor and his deputy. We'd barely got started when the publisher interrupted. He took over and threw me completely for a loop. He wasn't interested in my Games coverage, he wanted to talk about you.'

We were all listening intently and I saw Kate's hands were twitching slightly.

'He gave me the grilling of my life,' Sandra said. 'He'd already asked me for a report – I hope you won't be offended, but I sent them a full account of everything that was going on and what rubbish it all was - but he wanted more.

'He wanted every detail. He went on and on. I thought he was never going to stop. He quizzed me for about twenty minutes then finally he just said, 'Excellent. Thank you Miss Snow. Would you tell Kate that her funding will be reinstated with immediate effect.' He said the board would be meeting to ratify the decision, but you could be assured it will go through. Then he said, 'Oh and Miss Snow, Welcome Aboard.' Then the editor came back on, and didn't have much choice but to offer me the job.'

Kate didn't speak for a moment then she manipulated her sling and gave Sandra an awkward hug.

'You probably won't ever make anyone happier in your life,' she said, 'I really don't know how to thank you.'

Sandra grinned. 'You could have made my life hell when I arrived, but you let me get on with the job. That's thanks enough.'

They chatted for a while and when Sandra started to circulate, I took Kate aside and gave her a more gentle hug and a congratulatory kiss.

'You look as though you've gone into hovercraft mode,' I said, 'I'm so happy for you but I presume this means we won't be going to Norfolk.'

'We certainly will,' Kate said, without hesitation, 'we have to talk about our future. Ocean Reports can wait a few days.' She smiled. 'Anyway, you've been celibate too long.' She tapped the sling. 'We'll have to use a little ingenuity.'

We were back to 'our future' again, but she was so excited I couldn't tell what she had in mind. In spirit, she was not actually on the ground, and I decided to just let her ride the wave and worry about it later.

The terrace was nearly full now, and it looked as though I was going to be able to enjoy the party after all. Lottery was sharing a quiet moment with Clara, so I went over to Tim and Rachel to tell them the news. We had just started chatting when I saw Frampton waving to us to come into the house. He made the same signal to Lottery, who reluctantly left Clara alone at the bar, and we all went indoors.

'There's been an explosion on board the *Jurassic Star*,' Frampton said, 'all hell's broken loose on the marina.'

We went quickly into the room where Jay was monitoring the CCTV. He had set up a split screen with views from both ends of the quay. A fire was burning in the stern and four men were already on board with extinguishers, fighting to stop the blaze from spreading. People on other boats were watching anxiously and preparing to stave off the flames.

'I just hope the Fire Brigade can get through the crowds,' Frampton said.

A fire engine did arrive within minutes and the fire was quickly extinguished.

'They could have started a much bigger fire than that,' Tim said, 'they must know we're not on board. They want to draw us down there.'

'Well, no-one is going down there until we've checked the area. If they're waiting for you, we'll have a chance to pick them up.'

Frampton hesitated. 'I need to be there,' he said, 'can I have your word that you'll stay here until I give you the all clear.'

I assured him we would and when he had gone, we huddled round Jay's screen and watched the firefighters cleaning up the mess.

'You know what's going to happen, don't you?' I said.

'They're going to catch someone fairly soon,' Tim said.

'Yep,' Lottery said, 'I'll give it half an hour, at most.'

I went out onto the terrace and found Kate talking to a huge weather-beaten man who was explaining the peculiar currents of the Portland Race. This, I learned, was Mike Lano, Bouncer's trawlerman father, who was flirting outrageously with Kate. He was being closely observed by his equally rugged looking wife. Mrs Lano appeared to be used to her husband's ways but I guessed there would be limits and that if he went too far, she would have no trouble in bringing him to heel.

Kate was clearly amused by the attention and it took me a few minutes to insert myself and whisper news of the explosion.

'How much damage?' she asked. 'What about our kit?'

'I don't think it's too bad, but we can't to go down yet to check.'

I got her another drink and left Rachel to keep an eye on her while I went back to join Tim and Lottery.

Lottery's guess of half an hour was pretty close. Forty-five minutes later, Frampton came back in triumph.

'We've got them, both of them,' he said. 'It was Sanders and Waugh. They're safely in custody.'

'How did you catch them?' Tim asked.

'We were lucky. Someone reported seeing a man acting suspiciously just across from the marina. A detective went to investigate and recognised Sanders. Waugh was nearby. It looks as though Vossler's bottled it and left the dirty work to them.'

Tim glanced at Lottery but left it to me to say what we were all thinking.

'Inspector,' I said, 'I think we are probably still in an ambush situation.'

Frampton was clearly surprised. 'What makes you think that? Surely Vossler isn't going to carry on with his men locked up.'

'I'm sorry,' I said, 'but this has all been too easy. First of all, the fire was too small to be a serious attack. Secondly, Sanders has had a lot of experience. He was never going to be caught 'acting suspiciously' near the scene.'

Tim nodded. 'Sanders has served in Northern Ireland. He's done plenty of urban stake-outs. He'd never be that careless.'

'Chances are you were supposed to get them,' Lottery said.

'But why would they let themselves be caught? They're going to be charged with arson.'

'My guess is they are being sacrificed,' Tim said, 'and they probably don't even know it. Someone tipped you off deliberately so we would feel it was safe to get back down there.'

'You're saying there are still people waiting for you by the boat?'

'Not necessarily by the boat,' Tim said, 'in fact, almost certainly not.'

'Why not?'

'Tim pointed to Jay's screen. 'Marina security is on full alert. Your men are down there, so is the Fire Service. It's no place for an ambush.'

This thinking came as naturally to Tim and Lottery as breathing. I glanced at Birdy. He knew it too and neither of us needed to say a word.

'They almost certainly know that we're here at your house,' Tim said. 'That incendiary device was probably planted on the *Jurassic Star* much earlier. Someone has been watching us ever since Vossler left London.'

'You mean there's someone near the house.'

'That's where I would be if I was tasked for this,' Lottery said.

'But we've got police all over the area and when we checked ourselves, there was nothing suspicious.'

'No disrespect, Inspector, but I think Lottery and I should still take a look round,' Tim said.

'If someone has set a trap, they'll see you.'

'No they won't,' I said. 'Tim has been an SAS sniper. He instructs in concealed movement at Hereford and he's long since taught Lottery everything he knows. You wouldn't see them if they crawled through your vegetable patch while you were watering.'

Frampton still looked doubtful, then after a long pause, he reached his decision.

'Alright. Go take a look. You have my agreement.'

They had both come prepared. Tim was wearing a dark shirt and trousers. Lottery was wearing one of the brightly-coloured, glittery shirts he always wore for parties, but took it off to reveal a deep navy t-shirt.

Jay made a final check to make sure their cell-phones were secure and we agreed that I would stay close to Frampton to relay any messages.

The Inspector grew increasingly nervous as the preparations continued and he looked particularly uneasy when Tim produced a tin of camouflage cream to darken their faces.

Tim gave him a reassuring smile and the two men slipped out into the night.

We didn't hear from them for nearly thirty minutes, then Tim called in.

'We've found him,' he said. 'It's Ray Vossler himself. He's not close to the house and there's no immediate danger. Lottery's got him pinned down, and we think he's got an accomplice. Can you ask Frampton if he knows who lives at 44 Meadowcroft Way.'

'Where the hell is Vossler?' Frampton said when I passed on the message.

'Inspector, let them do it their way,' I said. 'If Tim says Lottery has got Vossler pinned down, then he has. Please, tell me about this house.'

'It belongs to Bill and Mabel Westerham, but they're in Tenerife.'

I passed the answer back to Tim.

'That's what I thought,' he said. 'There's a man sitting alone on the decking. He's got a beer in his hand, but he's not drinking it. There's a BMW parked in the drive and the gates are open. The car wasn't there before and there are no lights on in the house. I think it's Vossler's getaway driver.'

I relayed this to Frampton.

'The Westerhams don't have a BMW,' he confirmed.

I passed message to Tim.

'Understood,' he said, 'I'll deal with him.'

I could see Frampton was really worried now as he felt less and less in control.

We waited for Tim's next call, but instead, he reappeared at the house.

'All Ok so far, we've secured the man with the BMW.'

'What do you mean secured?' Frampton said.

Tim grinned. 'I made a sort of citizen's arrest. I grabbed him before he could communicate with Vossler.'

'Where is he now?

'I've handed him over to the Sergeant Phillips. He's holding him in a police car.'

'Are you sure he's involved?'

'We've got the right man,' Tim said. Phillips questioned him and he couldn't get into what was supposed to his own house and knew nothing about the area. And he's military alright. Bloody idiot has practically got his whole service record in his tattoos! Phillips will hold him till we've got Vossler.'

'Where exactly is Vossler?' Frampton said. 'How the hell did my men miss him?'

'He's very well hidden,' Tim said. 'He's in the hedge on the far side of the kitchen garden area. He's in a very professional military hide. You can bet he didn't build it himself. Probably the guy with the BMW did it.'

'So how do we get him?' Frampton said.

'I think you should let us take care of it,' Tim said. 'Lottery is very close to him. That's why he hasn't been communicating. Vossler's almost certainly got some kind of weapon and if you follow your rules, you'd have to call an Armed Response Unit. That will take time. I think we can get him without any problem.'

'Are the guests in danger?'

'I don't think so. He's a good way from the house and he can't see onto the terrace. He's watching the driveway. I'm pretty sure his plan is to wait until John and Kate drive away, then probably throw some kind of explosive device at them while he reaches the getaway car in the confusion.'

'This is very risky,' Frampton said, uncertainly.

'Tim's right, Inspector,' I said. 'If you call in an Armed Response Unit, there's no telling what he'll do.'

'It's a helluva gamble,' Frampton said. 'We can't have any heroics.'

Tim smiled. 'Inspector, we don't do heroics.'

'Alright,' Frampton said finally, 'it may cost me my job but I'll let you go ahead.'

I looked out over the terrace and thought how surreal the situation was. The evening really was running on two entirely separate levels. Outside, the party had warming up. Kate had become the centre of attention and I had never seen her look happier. The area close to the bar had become an impromptu dance floor and more and more couples were swaying to the music.

Inside, we were planning a military operation that, with luck, would finally put an end to our troubles. Everything was set for Tim to re-join Lottery and grab Vossler. It should have been a smooth, seamless operation, of the kind both men had carried out many times before – but that was not how it ended.

We were able to reconstruct the detail of what actually happened only some time later, and it turned out to be a mixture of high drama and farce.

The one factor we had overlooked in our planning was the raging hormones of a 19-year-old off-duty constable, a local lad, called Steve Wentworth, who had spent weeks trying unsuccessfully to bed a girl called Jenny, who he had known since school.

Using a mixture of charm and alcohol, Steve had finally persuaded Jenny to slip quietly upstairs with him, ignoring the ropes and signs Kath had posted to confine the party to the ground floor. The seduction successfully consummated, Steve had gone to the attic window for a breath of air. At that exact moment, Vossler had found the discomfort of the hide too much and had tried to stretch his cramped limbs. Feeling powerful after his sexual triumph, Steve had shouted loudly, in his best, newly-acquired police voice, 'Oy you, what do you think you're doing!'

As we had all predicted, Vossler panicked and tried to run. The next shout was a warning cry of 'Grenade!' from Lottery as he brought Vossler to the ground. Two seconds later, there was a loud explosion and earth and debris showered over the vegetables in the kitchen garden.

As Lottery immobilised Vossler, the final surreal touch was an angry shout from Kath.

'Andy, arrest that bloody man. He's blown up my chickens!'

19

Three days later, I was telling the story to Bob Cronin in the atrium of his Norfolk bridge club. Leslie had paid for a private ambulance to bring him home and Kate had gone with them, admitting reluctantly that her shoulder would make the Tiger Moth much too uncomfortable. I had just joined them after a trip to London for my first proper contact with MI6, a formal interview with the Chief, Sir Jeremy Peacock.

When I arrived, Kate had gone to the boatyard for what she had called wryly her 'proficiency test', a short sail with the owner of the yacht we were chartering, to establish whether she could sail it with one arm. 'I could probably sail it with my teeth,' she said as she left me with Bob, 'but I can see why he's be worried. It is a nice little boat.'

I was still in the dark about what Kate had in mind for 'our future.'

'Let's leave it till we're on board,' was all she would say. I wanted to quiz Bob to see if he had been given any hints but he wanted to hear first about Weymouth and Vossler.

When I told him about the chickens, Bob didn't laugh. 'It wouldn't have been as funny if Vossler had managed to throw a grenade at you lot instead,' he said seriously.

'I admit we were lucky,' I said, 'but he didn't get us, and that grenade has finally finished him. Now Ivan and Mark are back in Washington and Ray is back in prison, bail denied, with trial set for December.'

'What about Alvarez?'

'He's gone back to the States too and Maxine Herald is about to be charged with domestic slavery, so that should shut her up for a while.'

'What else has been going on?' Bob asked, 'Leslie only lets me find out bits and pieces.'

'Well, you're looking ten times better, so Leslie must be doing a great job of looking after you,' I said.

'Never mind that,' Bob said, impatiently, 'just tell me what's been going on, before he gets back.'

'Grayling is doing a brilliant job. Every day something positive about us is coming out in the national press and social media is falling into line beautifully. UpstairsBackstairs has gone quite quiet. I suspect someone with a stern face and an unusual warrant card has been over to Dublin to have a quiet word.'

'So everyone is OK?'

I ticked off the list.

'Tim is fine. His enquiry has been cancelled and his reputation is well on the way to being restored. Rachel is fine too and already back at work. Birdy hasn't seen his CO yet, but he's not too worried and his girlfriend is back from Singapore. Chunk is still in limbo, but he thinks he will manage to stay in the army.'

'And Lottery is the hero of the hour,' Bob said.

I laughed. 'Yes, but he's also the lonely bachelor of the hour. Clara has dumped him once and for all.'

'I thought she'd have been all over him.'

'We all did, but she wasn't impressed. According to Lottery her last words were, 'I'm not getting tied up with someone who's daft enough to rugby tackle a man who's about to throw a fucking grenade.'

This time Bob did laugh. 'Poor Lottery, he tries so hard to be a lover as well as a fighter!'

'It's Marie I'm most worried about,' I said, 'I think I've found a way to help her, but I can't get in touch with her.'

'What can you do? Bob said, 'the law isn't your world at all.'

'No, you're right, but Sir Alastair has offered to help. I told him the whole story: what happened in the Auberge, the teasing, the drone, everything.'

I didn't add what Marie had said to me in the Osmington churchyard, although that was what I had thought about the most since she had left.

'And he was sympathetic?'

'He was amused but also angry that the Vosslers could use social media to do so much damage. Anyway, you know what a gentleman he is and he's come up with a plan.

'There's a big dinner coming up, the most prestigious event in the legal calendar, apparently. Alastair has offered to invite Marie and all her future associates to be guests at his table. He's legal royalty and it would be a tremendous boost for them.'

'But you can't get hold of her?'

'I've left messages on her voicemail, but she hasn't replied yet.'

'Knowing Alastair, he'll find her,' Bob said, 'but the big question is: what about you and Kate?'

'To be absolutely honest, I have no idea,' I said. 'Kate keeps talking about 'our future' but won't spell anything out until this sailing trip. Has she said anything to you?'

'Not a word. What do you think she wants?'

'There's really only one kind of future she can want,' I said. 'She's never going to give up sailing. That's completely out of the question. What I think she might suggest is for me to live in the States and find a job not too far from Gloucester, Massachusetts, so I could be her 'home base' between trips.'

'Do you love her enough to do that?'

'When we were together in the States, it was absolutely wonderful,' I said. 'It did feel as though we were in love.'

'And now?'

'I'm not sure how real our time in Gloucester was. Kate's a difficult woman to get close to and all the stuff in Weymouth hasn't exactly helped. I don't really know how she feels now. But she did risk her life to save mine and that has to mean something.'

'If the idea of working in the States interests you, I'm sure I could help,' Bob said. 'There are plenty of universities, companies or other organisations that could use your knowledge of the Middle East. I could get you head-hunted, but do you really want that?'

'It's tempting,' I said, 'but there's still MI6. Chunk was right, Sir Jeremy Peacock is imaginative. My first interview with him went really well. He didn't make any specific promises but he said he was sure he could find something interesting for me to do if I wanted to return to the Service.'

I smiled. 'It's ironic. A week ago, I didn't have any prospects at all and now I seem to have at least two options.'

I wasn't finding the conversation at all comfortable. It was showing me how unsure I was about what I did want, but before Bob could press me on which option I favoured, Kate appeared through the door. The huge sling looked less incongruous in her sailing gear and she was smiling broadly.

'I passed,' she said, 'the *Water Lily* awaits. Thirty footer, gaff-rigged. I could have handled her when I was six, well perhaps seven. Sailing her is child's play.'

She turned to Bob. 'Before we begin our holiday, I'm going to take John for a little trip round the broad,' she said. 'Is it OK if we eat here tonight and set off tomorrow?'

'Of course,' Bob said, 'it's probably as well to try out that shoulder properly, just in case.'

I knew that wasn't what she had mind and I followed her down to the quay wondering whether I wanted an afternoon's sailing on the Norfolk Broads to decide my future.

The *Water Lily* certainly looked a lot easier to handle than the *Nova Scotia* and my only task was to cast off. Once on board, Kate took over completely and I could see she wanted to prove to herself, and to me, that the shoulder wasn't a problem.

She set the sails and we headed out across the broad, weaving between small cruisers and other pleasure yachts until we had rounded a headland and were out of sight of the bridge club.

'Where are we going?' I asked.

Kate smiled. 'We're not going anywhere. We're going to moor in that inlet over there. It should be quiet enough.'

'You mean quiet enough to talk,' I said, as we glided through a narrow gap in the reeds. I was suddenly quite nervous. It was happening too quickly. I didn't know what I wanted to say.

'No talk,' she said, 'just sex. I told you, you've been celibate long enough.'

'What about your shoulder?'

'To hell with my shoulder, three arms are better than none, right? Come and help me drop anchor.'

I was glad of the reprieve but I was uneasy too about the sex she had planned. When we were safely moored in the inlet, I saw Kate was also nervous and we were both right. It simply didn't work. We had barely got beyond the first kiss when the pain kicked in and we both changed course. Yet what followed was almost better than her plan. We held each other and caressed with a warmth and tenderness that had been missing since our Gloucester holiday.

'Was it this painful while you were sailing?' I said.

'Bloody agony!'

'Why didn't you say?'

'I would never admit I couldn't sail,' she said, 'but I'm really sorry about the sex. I thought if I concentrated, it would be like sailing and I wouldn't let it distract me from making love to you.

'It doesn't matter at all.'

As I said it I realised she was crying, and that it did matter to her very much.

'It's my own fault. I've been taking the sling off and I think I've done some damage.'

I had never seen Kate cry. I held her close, trying not to aggravate the pain and waited for the sobbing to subside. Eventually she manoeuvred herself gingerly round to face me.

'I'm so sorry,' she said, 'I had it all prepared. I was going to give you the experience of a lifetime and now I've messed it up. I wanted you to have something to...', she broke off suddenly.

'To what?'

'To remember me by.'

I had known from the first tears what was coming.

'So no future to discuss?' I said quietly. 'Is this what you planned to say all along?

'Oh no. When I suggested Norfolk, I was going to ask you to come the States.'

'And be your home base?'

'I suppose. I thought about it all the time while I was in hospital but I realised finally it was ridiculous, a fantasy. I'm hopeless at relationships. When I'm at sea, I never think about sex, or marriage or stuff like that. I'm focused every waking moment on the sea and the wind. When I come ashore, I see what other people have, the love and affection and friendship and I think, 'how nice that is.'

She touched my cheek.

'We are so good together, but it could never work. The truth is, I'm married already – married to the sea. There's a lovely shanty that says it all.'

She began to sing softly. It was another first. I had never seen her cry and never heard her sing. Though it was a shanty, she sang it softly, with a delicate, lilting tone.

The waves they are so wonderful,
And sailors' lives are free.
We sail the seas without a care,
And where she takes us there we'll be,
Out on the open sea.
A sailor's life is free from strife,
He knows no house or family,
He's married to the sea.

'The he can also be she,' she said, when she had finished.

Then suddenly she was business-like again. Drying her tears with the back of her hand, she said, 'help me get my sling on properly, it's your turn to sail.'

'Where are we going now?'

'Back to the bridge club. Just for once, I'm going to admit defeat and rest this bloody shoulder.'

She showed me how to use a paddle to push the boat back into open water. I hoisted the sails and she sat beside me, helping me navigate between the few craft still on our stretch of water.

'We've had some wonderful times,' I said, 'and you also managed to save my life. I shan't ever forget that.'

'I was the skipper,' she said, 'I had to look after my crew.'

I couldn't tell whether she was just making light of it or whether it really had been just the reflex of someone who took naturally to command. I think she realised my doubts and didn't want to answer the question in my mind. She said quickly, 'I'm glad it went well with MI6. Tell me more about the interview.'

'There isn't much more to tell. They will take me back. I haven't decided yet whether I want to go.'

'My place is on the ocean and yours is in Intelligence,' she said. 'You need a career, and they all say you're the best.'

She paused. 'And you also need a woman. Have you thought about Marie?'

This wasn't the moment to admit just how much I had thought about Marie.

I smiled. 'You've only just got rid of me. Isn't it a bit early to start match-making. Anyway I wasn't lying, there was nothing between us in France.'

'But there could be.'

'I doubt it.'

I thought of Osmington. This was one conversation I really wasn't ready for, but Kate persisted.

'Don't be so sure. Why don't you talk to her?'

'She won't even reply to my calls.'

Kate raised her good arm.

'Why not try in person?'

I looked across the water. Marie was standing on the bridge club quay.

Kate touched my arm. 'Don't be angry. I'm not playing games. I only called her last night. I wanted to make up for being such a selfish cow.'

'This could be a serious mistake,' I said.

'Maybe, but she's here, isn't she? Give it a try.' Kate smiled.

'Anyway, you can be sure of one thing. Marie is one woman who'll never be married to the sea.'

ABOUT THE AUTHOR

Photo: Dominic Ennis

Norman Hartley was educated at Manchester Grammar School and Durham University.

He has spent his whole life writing – as a Reuters correspondent, newspaper reporter and feature writer, television script writer and BBC editor.

He has written four other thrillers, *The Saxon Network, The Viking Process, Shadowplay,* and *Quicksilver.* His work has been translated into twelve languages.

normanhartleybooks.com

About The Saxon Games

In my earlier thriller, *The Saxon Network*, I created a group of tough, resourceful individuals who could cope with most of the challenges that life could throw at them. For the sequel, I was looking for a worthy adversary and it occurred to me that social media could provide it. I have long been fascinated by the way powerful and influential people can be brought down by rumours, exaggerations and distortions on the Internet.

During a lifetime as a journalist, I have grown used to lies. I have listened to them in every kind of venue from a corporate board meeting to the United Nations. I have listened to spin doctors weaving grotesque untruths – despite the fact that they knew they were lying, and we knew they were lying. Now, the Internet has taken lying to a new level and anyone and everyone can be a spin doctor.

We also all know someone like my character, Heather Fenton. In everyday life, these gossips and malicious rumour-mongers are an irritating nuisance. With social media as their platform, such people are a much more serious menace.

In its most basic form, online lying can be simply the publishing of unsubstantiated, unchecked facts and versions of events on Twitter, Facebook and in Blogs. However, in my books, I try to look into the future, as well as at present reality, and I believe that websites like my fictitious UpstairsBackstairs are inevitably becoming a growing part of our lives. Every journalist knows the joke about a 'story that is too good to check', and the Internet has opened the way to a flood of such inventions.

However, my 'Network' does survive the social media onslaught. I am an optimist and there is so much entertainment, education and just sheer pleasure on the Internet that I am sure I am right to be so.

The relationship between John Saxon and Kate Allison, however, is harder to be optimistic about. On so many levels they are made for each other, yet in the real world – as in my fiction – it is difficult to see how they could make a life together, while preserving their personal dreams and ambitions.

Let us hope that, as John Saxon's adventures continue, he will have better luck!

ACKNOWLEDGEMENTS

My thanks are due to a number of people who have helped with the background to the book. Their expertise has been invaluable; any mistakes are my own. For details about security during the sailing section of the Olympic Games, I was guided by the Coxswain of the Weymouth Lifeboat, Andy Sargent, and its chief mechanic, Phil Hansford. Maritime journalist Laura Kitching was a splendid source information about reporting the Games and my sailing expert was Sidmouth-based international yachtsman, Tom Griffiths. My thanks, as always, to retired British Airways Captain, Clive Elton, for his advice on Tiger Moth flying and to Jonathon Savill, for all the naval and other titbits he keeps on providing, without even realising it. Finally, my special thanks to composer Vanessa Young, for permission to quote from her lovely sea-shanty, *Married to the Sea.*

68555925R00097

Made in the USA
Charleston, SC
10 March 2017